SPEAK FOR THE DEAD

A JOAN KAHN BOOK

SPEAK
FOR
THE
* _____ DEAD

Rex Burns

HARPER & ROW, PUBLISHERS

New York : Hagerstown : San Francisco : London

A HARPER NOVEL OF SUSPENSE

TO

Herb and Dot

1

Gabriel Wager was new to the homicide section of the Denver Police Department, and the partner who was to break him in had been sent to a three-week police seminar at Oklahoma State.

"We send people whenever we have the money, Wager; if we don't, we lose the opportunity." Chief Doyle's lower teeth shone briefly in what might have been a smile. The detectives called him "the bulldog" behind his back. "You've had a lot of experience over in narcotics, and you'll do all right here. *If* you meet deadlines, and *if* you follow proper procedures. We compete for funds with forty other agencies, and I don't want any black eyes for my section."

The deadlines were court orders interpreting Constitutional rights: seventy-two hours from arrest to advisement, one week from advisement to second appearance, preliminary within thirty days, and so on. Wager was a little peeved that Doyle didn't credit him with knowing basics. The crack about procedures was another thing; it was the unease a conventional cop always felt toward a narc agent, ex- or otherwise.

To make sure Wager would do all right, especially without a partner, the bulldog had assigned him to the midnight-to-eight shift—usually the quietest of the three. However, two days later, on Wednesday morning, October 20th, a known-dead report came in at 7:10. When Wager took it, he guessed Doyle would want him to leave it for the day shift, due on in less than an hour; but Wager was a cop, and he knew he was as good as any other. He tossed aside the procedure manual he had been leafing through and hustled across town in that little pause of traffic that comes before the morning rush.

By the time he pulled in to the parking area above the Botanic Gardens, an overcast October dawn was seeping into the sky, bringing the kind of gray that made things visible without casting any shadows at all. In the dull light, the conservatory looked like a glass balloon held to earth by cold threads of concrete. The only other vehicle in the narrow parking lot was the police car responding to the call. A patrolman sat with his legs dangling out of the front seat to speak tersely on the radio. He nodded hello as Wager approached. "You the new homicide detective?"

"Gabe Wager. What do you have?"

The officer's chrome name badge said "G. Bauman." "You got to see it to believe it, Detective Wager." Turning back a page or two in his pocket notebook, he read the specifics of the reported death. "The victim was found inside the conservatory building; a white female, age probably between twenty and twenty-five. No identification."

"She was found inside?" Wager had assumed the body would be lying in a thicket handy to one of the roads surrounding the grounds.

"Yeah. That surprised me, too. Anyway, she's got short blond hair, blue eyes, and no identifying marks or scars. She was found by the chief utility worker, a Mr. Salvador Solano, address 1325 Ulster, Denver.

2

He was just beginning his work when he found it."

"Does he always come in about this time?"

Bauman looked up, the straight brown hair swinging far beneath the edge of his cap. In Wager's day, an officer had regulations about the length of his hair. "I don't know. He's in the janitor's room with my partner. He's pretty shook up still, so I didn't ask him too much."

"Cause of death?"

"I sure as hell don't think it was suicide. The lab people are on their way, and I just gave the medical examiner another call."

"Any indications of assault? Rape?"

"Nope." A tiny smile said Bauman was holding back a surprise.

Wager didn't like coyness, especially in cops who were supposed to gather information and pass it to the proper authority. At a death scene, the homicide detective was the proper authority. "Was she dressed or was she naked? Did she die here or was she brought here dead?"

"She was brought here—she sure was. But I don't know about her clothes."

"Then she was naked."

"I don't know."

"Goddamn it, Bauman, she's either wearing clothes or not!"

"Yeah. But we don't know which. There was nothing to put the clothes on."

"What do you mean?"

"All we found was her head."

2

Salvador Solano, forty-three years old, was less than Wager's medium height, had dark eyes and hair showing gray at the temples. He hopped up from his thermos of coffee when Wager and Bauman came into the small janitor's office tucked beneath a stairwell that rose from the dark lobby.

"This is Detective Wager," Bauman said. "My partner, Bill Haraway; this here's Mr. Solano."

"Hi," said Haraway. "Did Gene show it to you yet?"

Gene must be the "G." in Officer Bauman's name. "No. Were you the only person to go in there, Mr. Solano?" Wager asked.

"Me and the two officers, yeah. Yes, sir." He sat a little straighter and looked at Wager like a schoolboy waiting for questions.

"Want to tell me what happened?"

He took a deep breath and Wager could see that the events were sorting themselves into a story. In a few days, it would be worth a beer at a local bar and not worth a squeaky fart to an investigator. "Like I told the officer, here, I came in like I always do and turned on the lights and started the water and checked the gauges."

"Gauges?"

"Temperature, humidity. They're supposed to be computerized and all, but I still keep an eye on them. There's a lot of expensive specimens here, and it wouldn't take much to kill some of them. So I watch the gauges just in case. Even if it ain't my job."

"What'd you do next?"

"Like always, I went to turn on the misting system and then started my cleanup. I rake the walks to get paper and stuff out of the plants. That part ain't so bad. Most people who come here are pretty good about using the trash cans. Even most of the kids, though school trips are something else—you get a bunch of kids on a school trip and half the time they don't give a darn for anything, you know?"

"How did you find the head, Mr. Solano?"

"Well, I was raking the side path up by the big waterfall, and I thought I saw something across the stream, a paper bag or something. There's this little stream that starts at the big waterfall on the west end and goes all the way down the conservatory. Well, I looked across and when I did, I saw it. Her."

"What'd you do then?"

"Nothing. It was really weird. I mean, I knew what it was right away—my eyes told me what it was. But my mind wouldn't believe it. I thought it was maybe a picture or part of a statue—one of them kind in the store windows, a dummy, you know. Then I saw where it bled. And I guess I stood there about five minutes just thinking, It's real."

"What then?"

"I backed right out. No, I must of turned around to get down here to the lobby—that's where the telephone is, just over there—but I don't remember walking. I called the operator and she called the cops. I couldn't even dial the emergency number, just the operator. I can't even remember what I said to her. She told me to stay here and she would call the cops."

"We got the dispatch at"—Bauman flipped a page of his notebook—"six-forty-four."

"Was the building secure when you got here this morning?" Wager asked Solano.

"Yeah, I guess. The door I always use was locked, anyway, and I had to unlock the front doors to let the cops in. That's the only two ways in here."

"Why don't you show me the door you used?" Wager said.

Solano led him and Haraway across the echoing lobby. In the room's still air, the heavy fragrance of a dahlia display reminded Wager of a warm funeral parlor. "It's back here." A concrete slab spouted a shelf of water that plunged into a long reflecting pool surrounded by the bright dahlias. Behind it, a bronze-framed glass door opened on a small landing beneath the overhang of the roof.

"Why do you use this door?"

"It's the employee door—I'm an employee. Our parking lot's just down there." He pointed left past the loading ramp to a series of greenhouses separate from the domed building. A bank of earth hid the greenhouses from the main grounds. A single red Toyota pickup with a white camper shell sat next to the first greenhouse.

"The truck's yours?"

"Yeah. I always park there."

Because it's the employee parking lot. Wager knelt to peer closely at the door's metal frame. "This was locked when you got here?"

6

"Like always."

It was a dead-bolt latch, a double cylinder that required a key inside and out, and could not be opened with a sliver of stiff plastic. The weathered bronze frame showed no tool scratches or dimpled marks. If it had been picked, the lab people would spot the inevitable scratches on the tumblers. If not, then someone had used another door—or a key. "Do all the employees have a key to the outside doors?"

"I'm not sure how many people got keys. Me and a few others."

"How many people work here?"

Solano thought a moment. "About twenty-three. There's more in the summer—outside help. But not all of them have keys; most are people who don't come in here to work."

"Who keeps a record of the keys?"

"That would be Mr. Sumner, the deputy director. He keeps a record of everything. He's that way—everything's got to be on a chart, you know?"

Wager knew. He jotted the name in his green notebook. "You feel up to showing it to me now?"

Solano's breath whistled in his hairy nostrils. "I guess. This way."

Wager followed the nervous man into the lobby and through another bank of glass doors. All but one were locked, and all of the locked ones were dead bolt also. "Is this always left open?" Wager nodded at the unlocked door.

The man scratched at his cropped hair. "It's supposed to be locked, but a lot of times it ain't. I really don't remember if I had to unlock it or not this morning."

"Does the same key fit these doors as fits the outside one?"

"Sure. They're all on the same master. If they weren't, we'd have a ring of keys this big!"

In the conservatory, tall palm trees loomed shaggy against the glass sky, and billows of leaves and branches rose on each side of the winding sand paths. The stream hissed and splashed from half a dozen hidden corners, and humid air clung to breathe different scents as the men wound past a variety of limbs and blossoms.

"This is really pretty," said officer Haraway. "Kind of like Eden."

Complete with snake, thought Wager. "Did you and Bauman look around for any other parts of the body?"

"Yes, sir," said Haraway. "In here we did. Some. But we didn't find anything. It was pretty dark and we stayed on the paths. We figured the lab people would make a systematic, so we just looked from the paths. If you want the outside grounds searched, we'll need more people. It's about the size of three city blocks."

"It smells like there's some more around," said Wager.

Solano sniffed. "That's an amorphophallus. It usually blooms in the spring, but it's got a little scent now." The utility worker's face grew pale and he swallowed. "It makes a smell like rotten meat to draw flies; I don't think I'm going to be able to work around that plant for a long time."

Wager did not like the odor either; he pointed up the slope of the curving path, "Come on, Solano, let's get it over with."

They passed under shiny oleander leaves and vines twisting up palm trunks to arc into a green matting that tumbled clusters of bougainvillaea. Here and there, air plants hung down their hairy tendrils. Small nameplates dangled beside each specimen; and Wager, still puzzling over how the head had got in there, gazed at the thick and breathing greenness and fragrant explosions of blossoms. And he began to puzzle over why as well.

They turned onto a smaller path that looped near a ribbon of water plunging six feet into the concrete-banked stream. "It's over there," Solano gestured without looking. "Just down from that fig tree."

Stooping to peer across the stream and under the broad leaf of an elephant-ear plant, Wager saw it lying on its cheek as if someone had placed it on its neck and wearily it had tilted to one side to lie on the moist, dark earth. The eyes were half open, the jaw hung slack to gap the mouth slightly. Against the gray, drained flesh, the make-up around the eyes and the lipstick were very dark. And in some strange way, the head did not seem out of place. The straight nose, the long but gently rounding curve of the jaw had a symmetry that made Wager understand why Solano might think it was from a mannequin; and if it had been marble instead of real, it might even be picturesque.

"Now that's something I didn't notice the first time," said Haraway.

"What?" asked Wager.

"The hair. See? Somebody must have combed the hair after they set it there."

He was right; the only disarray was where the earth had lifted the hairs as the head had sagged over. Wager could see the grooves of comb teeth still furrowing the sweeping bangs.

From the far end of the conservatory, Officer Bauman shouted above the splash of water, "Haraway? You and Detective Wager around here? The lab guy's coming."

Wager went down the short path to the juncture. A tired-looking man in a baggy corduroy coat leaned against the pull of a toolbox. Wager recognized Fred Baird; he had worked with him almost two years ago. "You all by yourself?"

"Hi, Gabe." Baird fought back a yawn as he shook hands. "We only have one man on this shift." The yawn won. "And I almost made it through without any crap tonight. Is the medical examiner here yet?"

"No. He's been called."

The lab technician nodded. "It'll take him awhile; mornings are a bad time. Where's the body?"

"There's only the head so far."

"Oh. God."

"It's this way. Me, the two officers, and the chief utility worker have been the only ones around. As far as I know, everyone's stayed on the paths."

"Right. I'll get things started before I go off duty. Ask Bauman to call for the day shift to cover me when they come on. I think this is going to be one long son of a bitch." He sighed and toted the heavy box after Wager.

"I'd like you to go over all the doors for any sign of forced entry," said Wager. "I didn't see anything, but maybe you can pick up something. And there's a lot of outside grounds."

"Right, right—all doors and windows, all avenues of approach. And tell the guy who found her that we'll need a set of his prints. But if you want the grounds searched, call the Uniformed Division. We don't have enough people to do the legwork *and* the lab work. We'll take a look at what they find." He peered past the shiny green fan of a palm leaf. "God, it doesn't look real, does it?"

"It's real."

"God."

Baird unslung a Speed Graflex and began popping blue flash bulbs, jotting a note after each shot, careful not to step in the soft earth off the packed grit of the path. His lips clamped tight as he aimed the camera. The man knew his business, and Wager was doing no good just standing around. He went in search of Mr. Solano and the two officers.

They were in a corner of the lobby lit by the glass doors of the main entry. Bauman, finishing a ciga-rette, was restless; Haraway—darker, shorter, and slightly younger—looked tired in the hard glare.

"Anything more you want of us, Detective Wager?"

"Just a copy of the offense report." It was homicide's problem now; the uniformed officers' shift was at an end, and there was a lot of paperwork left.

"We'll leave it with division this morning."

As they pushed through the heavy doors, Solano

clapped a hand to his forehead. "Holy cow! I forgot to check the water for the mosses!" He started for a corner of the conservatory.

"Hold it," Wager said. "I wish you wouldn't do anything until the lab people get finished."

"Oh boy—Mr. Sumner's not gonna go for that."

Mr. Sumner wouldn't have a damned thing to say about it—the area was a crime scene, and the police had full authority. "I'll explain things to him," said Wager.

"You think I better call him about this? He really won't like cops stomping around in the specimens. Yeah," Solano answered his own question, "he'll be up by now; I better call him." He went to the lobby telephone.

"Fine. Then I want to ask you a few more questions."

Solano made his call and hung up the phone. "He said he'd be right down. He really sounded upset. He told me not to let anybody do anything until he gets here." The man's brown eyes looked toward the conservatory. "You think it's O.K. to let that laboratory guy mess around in there?"

"He'll be real careful, Solano. Have you showed me all the doors? There's no other way to get into the conservatory?"

"There's the balcony doors up there. But you have to come in through the lobby here. That's the stairs." He pointed to the sloping ceiling that roofed the janitor's room. Over a ledge, Wager could see the glass of the upper doors. "There's this balcony on the other side, and a ramp leads down to ground level in the conservatory."

"Any other doors into the conservatory?"

"The west end has a set. But they're emergency doors and only open from the inside. And they got an alarm—a bell goes off if anybody opens them. Kids are all the time setting it off."

Wager would take a look at those later. "Are those more stairs to a third floor?"

"Yeah. The rooftop garden. It's for showing patio plants and such. You know, like people grow on their apartment balconies. But it's a dead end; that's the only stairs up to it."

"What's in there?" Wager pointed to the east wall of the lobby where large wooden doors with a little-used look hung shut.

"That's the education wing. The auditorium's through there, and over there's the library and herbarium," Solano said.

"Does it connect with the conservatory?"

"Only through here."

As Bauman had told him, the victim sure as hell hadn't walked here. "Windows? Any windows in the conservatory?"

"Sure, plenty. But they're all up on top."

"Could somebody open one from the outside?"

Solano's head wagged. "No way. They work off hydraulic pistons. I'll show you."

Wager followed Solano back into the humid greenness of the domed space. The shorter man pointed up to the roof where triangles of glass sat at the peak of the structure. Even if someone had climbed up from the outside, there was no way to descend. "That's a long way up," said Wager.

"Fifty feet. Even the sparrows have trouble getting in."

Wager studied the pages of the small notebook. "Was it crowded when the place closed yesterday?"

"I don't know. I get off at two-thirty or so. That's one of the nice things about this job—every afternoon's mine. And, heck, I never could sleep late anyway. Bad kidneys."

"Who locks up?"

"Depends on who goes home last. Usually it's Mauro. But Mr. Sumner can tell you. He's got a chart that says. Are you sure it's O.K. to let that guy mess around down there?"

"It's O.K." Wager strolled to the middle of the conservatory, heels crunching in the gravel, and looked at the variety of growing things surging up through the moist air. Why. And how. It wasn't likely that someone brought the head in just before the conservatory closed. It wasn't likely that entry had been through the emergency doors with their alarm system. It *was* likely that somebody used a key. Unless Baird came up with something that showed a lockpick, it was damned likely that someone used a key. "You live only a couple of miles away?" he asked Solano.

"Yeah. It's a short drive."

"Did you recognize the victim?"

"What?"

"Have you ever seen her before?"

"Good gosh, Officer, how could anybody tell? I didn't even think she was real, you know?"

"Well, do you know any women who fit the description: maybe twenty-five, short blond hair, regular features?"

"No. And I better not. The wife would be all over me."

"Thanks for your help." He watched Solano walk in his quick, nervous way toward the lobby doors. Then he searched for Fred Baird. The technician was dusting the smoothest tree trunks and larger branches around the area where the head rested.

"Have you got anything?" Wager asked.

"Not yet. Whoever put it here had to come this way—they couldn't reach across the stream." This way was down a steep bank past a cluster of banana trees, giant ferns, and a tall eruption of leaves. "Great God, look at the name of this plant." Baird giggled and pointed to the plastic tag beside the shooting green stalks. It said "Self-Heading Philodendron."

Wager didn't see anything to laugh at. He jotted the fact in his little book. "Any idea how long it's been there?"

"Hard to say. The M.E. can make a guess if he ever gets here."

Solano had arrived around 6:30; it was now a little past eight. "Two hours? Maybe less?" The utility worker could have brought it in with him and then "found" it.

"I'd say more—there's a lot of drainage under it. But you'd better ask the M.E." Baird stepped back and looked for other likely places a hand would rest. "I'll bet you're going to want us to survey this whole goddamned conservatory, aren't you?"

"I would like to know how it got here."

"Right. And why some son of a bitch would screw

up such a pretty place by bringing it here." He bent to dust another smooth tree trunk. "You want to call an ambulance? When the M.E.'s finished, it should go to the morgue for the pathologist. I sure as hell don't care to take it back in my car."

Besides, Doyle's procedure manual required corpses to be transported by suitable conveyance, and Wager supposed that meant bits and pieces as well. He keyed the G.E. radio pack holstered on his belt and sent the code for an ambulance, no siren necessary. "The deputy director's coming down," he told Baird. "He's worried about his bushes and stuff."

"Right. And I'm worried about knocking off. Is that day shift on its way?"

"Bauman said he called." The conservatory's shadows had faded to reveal, here and there among the towering palm trees, pink and white flowering vines and pulpy clusters of purple banana sprouts. This was the upper end of the area; the lobby was down at the east end where the stream fed a dark still pool whose bottom glinted with pennies and dimes. He half wondered if one of the coins had been tossed by whoever brought the head.

Wager walked back around to the side path across the stream from the head. The face showed no bruises, no contortions, none of the knotted, frozen cords and sinews that came with agony. Instead, it seemed to have eased its life away in one long, gentle breath as if sighing at the glossiness of leaves, the richness of shoots and tendrils and moist protruding roots, the sudden flame of birds of paradise. There was a reason for it. He had been a cop long enough to know there was always a reason, even when no sane mind could understand it. This was not an easy place to get into, and most killers would dump a whole body. The person or persons unknown had gone out of their way to put just the head here, Wager figured, knowing it would be found within hours. And they'd done it because it was important to them. It was something worth taking such a chance for, something that had a reason for them.

Wager no longer saw the gray skin or the heavy leaves glinting in the pale light. In his mind, he held side by side the living green of plants and the dead flesh of the head. The two things together meant something.

A clatter at the lobby doors pulled him back; the day shift of lab technicians came in followed by a tall Anglo whose white hair still sprouted sleep in ruffled thrusts. Behind him, very quiet, Solano chewed his lip. The white-haired man, who must have been Sumner, talked loudly over the echo of the stream: "These are very delicate specimens—they shouldn't be disturbed at all, and I'm quite upset that your people pursued their activities without first checking with me!"

The lead technician from the day shift, new to Wager, bent to gaze at the head, then grunted to Baird, "Morning. Why don't you go get some breakfast?"

Fred snorted something like a laugh and began packing his kit. "Right. Breakfast. I'll just go, thanks. The M.E.'s been called, my samples are over there, I've dusted the immediate area. Good-bye."

"What's this powder on my bignoniacea?" Sumner pointed to a tree trunk.

"It's fingerprint powder—like talcum powder," answered Baird. "Nothing toxic: will not harm, will not stain. It'll rinse right off."

"But it will get into the soil!"

"It's magnesium silicate and aluminum—hardly enough for a trace."

"How much more do you intend to throw around?"

Baird snapped the hasp on his kit. "Maybe some on the doors, but that should be it. These gentlemen would like to search the area systematically and look for footprints, cigarette butts, that sort of thing. Most of the search will be along the paths."

"But that's where we place our choice growth! We have over six hundred specimens, and many are extremely delicate!"

Wager stepped forward. "They'll be real careful, Mr. Sumner."

The second of the two lab men nodded. "We'll take good care, sir. I'm a plant freak myself. Ferns. Love 'em."

"Well, yes, the asplenia are very nice, but . . ."

"And," added Wager, "we wouldn't want to leave any hands or feet lying around, now, would we?"

"Oh. Oh my. I didn't think of that." Sumner's round eyes of anger turned into round eyes of horror. He peered this way and that among his plants.

"Let's go back to the lobby, Mr. Sumner. Maybe you can answer a few questions for me," said Wager.

"Questions?"

"About the routine of locking up the place and

such."

"Ah, well, that's usually Mauro's job. Dominick Mauro. He's the senior assistant utility worker."

"Was he the one to lock up last night?"

"I believe so; I'll have to look at the charts to be certain. He should be here at ten."

That would be unauthorized overtime—without pay. It would piss off the police union, but there wasn't anything in the bulldog's procedure manual against pissing off the police union. Which Wager sort of enjoyed doing anyway. "Solano is the one who comes early?"

"Yes." Sumner relaxed for the first time, and it made his white hair look incongruous against the sudden youthfulness of his lean face. Wager guessed he was a little past fifty, but his hands moved like those of a younger man. "We're very fortunate with those two: Salvador doesn't like to sleep late, and Nick doesn't like to get up early." The tension came back. "They're both very trusted and long-time employees, Inspector. State employees."

"Yes, sir. Do any other employees have keys to the outside doors?"

"Keys? I was just looking at the key chart the other day. . . . We have very few keys that unlock the outer doors. I have one. The conservatory superintendent, Mr. Weimer, has one. And the chairman of our board of trustees. Though I don't think he's ever used it. Oh, yes, there's the emergency key that's kept in Greenhouse One. That makes six."

"What's the chairman's name?"

"Mr. Klipstein. Gerald Klipstein." Sumner frowned.

"He and his wife are in Europe. When he returns, he's going to be quite upset about all this."

"Who can get to the emergency key?"

"The senior gardeners. They have the keys to the greenhouses, and the emergency key's in a locked cabinet."

"What's the names of these gardeners?"

"Leon Duncan and Joe Mazzotti. Both very fine men; they've both been here since the nineteen-fifties. I can look it up on the longevity chart."

"That's O.K., Mr. Sumner. You went home earlier than Mauro last night?"

"Unless we have a special evening function, Mr. Weimar and I go home around four. The buildings and grounds close promptly at four-forty-five."

"What kind of evening functions do you have?"

"Oh, previews for our members, occasional night classes, slide presentations. We're really quite active when the sun goes down, ha, ha."

"Yes, sir. But there was nothing going last night?"

"No, Inspector. There was 'nothing going,' as you say."

"Have you ever seen the victim before?"

"Good Lord—I didn't even glance at it! I have no idea what it looks like, and I really don't want to!"

"Could I have your address? In case I've got more questions later."

"Certainly." Sumner gave the street address of the gardens' administration building as well as his un-listed home telephone number. His home address was, like Solano's, within a long walking distance of the gardens, though in a southern direction toward the Denver Country Club.

"Is that all, Inspector? I'm afraid the press will make a field day of this, and I've got to warn the trustees."

As Sumner let himself out the main entrance, Wager saw the ambulance crew heaving a rubber-tired stretcher over the locked turnstile of the picket fence. The two attendants puffed toward him. "Where's the victim?"

"Through there," said Wager. "But the M.E. hasn't come yet. And you won't need that thing."

"Oh, yeah? Why?" The lead attendant was a stocky kid with cropped red hair and freckled arms that filled the short sleeves of the smock. A blue-and-orange shoulder patch said he had passed his Emergency Medical Technician's examination. The driver was a thin Negro with heavy oil holding his hair down in a slick crust.

"All we have so far is the head."

"No shit!" said Red. "Why in hell didn't somebody tell us that before we unloaded this thing? We had to haul it over that goddam gate to get it here."

"It's not something you put on the air," Wager said.

"Yeah? Well we got rubber bags for that kind of thing, you know? I mean these wagons are heavier'n hell and we didn't really need to unload it, did we?"

"It's down that way. You'll see the lab people."

"Jesus Christ. That's the trouble with everybody, they never think of nobody else. Come on, Ernie, let's run this fucker back." They swung the stretcher around and rammed it through the doorway. "Like I was telling you, Ernie, just once—just one time, man—I'd like to meet somebody that didn't just think of their own fucking self first. Just once!"

3

Wager reached the homicide office a little after nine with the list of people who had keys and with the slight headache he always got when he went too long without food. A team from the day shift, Ross and Devereaux, was finishing its paperwork before going on the street. When not working a homicide, the detectives were on call to help other sections of the Crimes Against Persons Division: stickup, assault, bunco, occasionally rape—though lately the politicians had given that section enough funding, and they preferred to use their own specially trained man-woman teams. And the bomb section was always on its own.

He took the dregs of night-shift coffee from the chrome cylinder in the hall and sighed as he slid behind the desk he shared with two other men. Already two of the names on the list of key-owners had been checked off: Klipstein, who was in Europe; and the conservatory director, Weimer, who was at a three-day conference in St. Louis. That left six names. Wager scraped at his eyelids with his thumbs and sipped the strong coffee, staring at the list without really seeing it.

"There's the overtime kid—Wager thinks he's still Supernarc." Detective Ross, completing a records-search application form, winked at his partner, another tall, thick-bodied man. At five eight, Wager

23

was half a foot shorter than any other member of the homicide section.

"Wager thinks he needs a cup of coffee and a little peace and quiet," Gabe said.

The partner, Devereaux, glanced up from his stack of papers. "Fred Baird told us you really got a good one."

"I'm glad he liked it. Did he have anything from the lab yet?"

Ross didn't try to hide his irritation. "No, he didn't have anything from the lab yet. He put in his time and he went home. You really do think you're a supercop, don't you?"

Wager guessed he had just broken a rule of the office by not kidding back. "No, Ross. I'm tired."

"Then knock off. You're not in narcotics any more; you don't have to make anybody think you're rupturing yourself for Mama and apple pie." Ross tugged his checked sport coat over his arms. "We do things different over here. But, by God, just as good. We got a goddamned good conviction rate in this section, and we didn't get it by being hyper—we got it by collecting the evidence!" He strode out of the office.

Devereaux, with a little embarrassed grin, paused a moment in the doorway. "Ross didn't sleep good again. Nightmares. You get them after a while; you know how it goes. Is there anything you want us to follow up on?"

"Not yet. Thanks."

"*Ciao.*"

Wager closed his burning eyes and slumped in the hard chair to hold the coffee mug under his nose.

The steam smelled better than the thick coffee tasted, and he inhaled deeply, feeling the rigid muscles in his neck begin to relax, listening to the rhythmic clatter of a distant teletype, the tinny rattle of telephones, voices male and female raised over the chatter from the records section just down the hall. On his desk, his portable radio popped and squawked with the business of District 2, the most active of the quadrangles that divided the City and County of Denver. All those noises added up to the familiar sounds of every division he'd worked, from street grunt to narcotics. And now homicide. It wouldn't take long to feel at home here. But Ross's words held some truth: the pace was slower, more methodical. In the narcotics section, you were part of the crime while it was taking place in order to have a case for court; the pace was always set by the bastard you wanted to bust. Here in homicide, you picked up the pieces after the crime was committed. If there were witnesses, you could move fast; if not, you could only go as fast as the evidence allowed.

But there was another reason behind Ross's anger; Wager knew Ross was threatened by Wager's putting in a little overtime. Here was Ross doing his eight hours and happy in his stride, when along comes a runty Hispano who strides a little faster and works a little harder. All of a sudden Ross has competition. Well, piss on him—Ross didn't have to compete unless he wanted to; and if he did, it was his worry. Because now homicide was as much Wager's home as anybody's.

He took another sip of bitter coffee and picked up the telephone; the drawling voice on the other end answered, "Lab, Hawkins."

"This is Wager in homicide. Do you have anything yet on that head found out at the Botanic Gardens?"

"Wager? You new up there?"

"Yes."

"Hey, that's a weirdo. It sure as hell doesn't give us much to work with. The dental-records check could run two weeks; maybe a month or more if she's from out of town. And if we're lucky."

"The team hasn't come back from the field yet?"

"No. They called in some uniformed people to go over the grounds. It'll take most of the morning to search the area—that's a big place. But we should have the morgue shots by this afternoon, so you'll have a little to work with. Too bad she didn't have fingers. We could get an I.D. in an hour if she had fingers."

"Yeah. Ain't that like a woman."

"Ha. Right."

Wager hung up and glanced at his watch: 9:45. His headache was worse, and whether he wanted it or not, he should put something into his stomach before going back to the Botanic Gardens to see Mauro. But Doyle stopped him in the hallway.

"You still here, Wager?"

It was a stupid question, and he hesitated a second too long before answering simply, "Yes, sir."

The bulldog's lower teeth shone; this time it definitely was not a smile. "Who's handling the thing that came in this morning?"

"I am."

It was the chief's turn to pause and he made it

longer than Wager's. "Maybe you'd better turn it over to Ross and Devereaux."

"It came in on my shift. I'm the officer of record." And Doyle's own procedure manual named the officer of record as the officer in charge.

"This isn't your basic, everyday snuff," Doyle said. "I've already had four calls from the press on it."

"I'm the officer of record," Wager said again.

The bulldog pulled his upper lip behind those lower teeth and made little chewing sounds. "So you are, Wager. So don't screw it up; I want a sound conviction on this one."

What the hell did he think Wager wanted? The combination of a headache and Doyle made him distrust his own mouth. He just nodded.

"If you need any help at all, you ask—understand? We get convictions because we work as a team. There are no prima donnas in the homicide section."

"If I wasn't any good, I wouldn't have been sent here." That was only partially true—he was also here because a federal Law Enforcement Assistance grant ran out and closed the special narcotics section; D.P.D. had to put him somewhere.

"Well, you better know that I took you on a trial basis, Wager, because I'm short-handed as hell. And you better know this, too: homicide isn't narcotics. You got a reputation for being an animal; if you screw up in my division, you're going to end up sitting at the information desk arranging tours for Boy Scouts."

"I'm a goddamned good cop."

"We'll find out. Just you remember: good cops get facts—they don't go around lumping people."

On his way to the Botanic Gardens, Wager drove slowly around the green lawns and clusters of blue spruce that formed Cheesman Park. It lay just west of the gardens across a winding street now emptied of the last clutter of rush-hour traffic. Tall iron bars and a padlocked gate whose rusty hinges were unused fenced this end of the gardens, and it wasn't until he swung up Eleventh Avenue that he glimpsed the crinkled glass of the conservatory through the towering apartments and expensive condominiums scattered along the edge of the grounds. He turned down the narrow end of Gaylord Street where it dead-ended at the north entrance, and pulled in beside Solano's red Toyota truck. Half a dozen other cars and pickups nosed against the wall of the detached greenhouses, and as Wager looked up the soaring arc of the conservatory, a uniformed officer plodded around the building to poke his arm cautiously into the pfitzers that sprouted along the foundation.

Earlier, when Wager had entered the grounds from the east entrance, he had hopped a locked turnstile in a low fence of metal pickets, the same one that gave the ambulance attendants so much trouble. But from this side, a gap between a chain-link fence and Greenhouse 1 opened onto a wide concrete apron; beyond that, a rose garden gave easy entrance to the main grounds. Behind him, across the alley, apartments and condominiums peered down; and half a block away towered a forty-floor column of staggered balconies. He could see few outside lights at this corner of the building; chances were that no one in the apartments had seen anybody enter last night.

But they would have to be questioned anyway. And that was something Ross could do—ask a hundred people if they saw anything last night.

Slipping through the gap between fence and greenhouse, Wager crossed the concrete apron. A policeman and three groundskeepers stood digging through a tall bin of compost. The officer looked up.

"This area's closed, mister. Go on back out."

"I'm Detective Wager from homicide." He didn't bother to show his shield; there was enough identification in his voice. "It looks like you haven't found anything."

"No, sir." The officer stamped first one shoe and then the other to shake clinging brown shreds from his trousers. "We've got one more bin to go through." There were eight of the tall, open squares, each half filled with mixtures that differed slightly in color and odor. "But if you ask me, it's a waste."

Wager hadn't asked. But everybody liked to get in on the act. "Why?"

"Well, if he brought the whole body here and cut off the head, there'd be a hell of a lot of blood somewhere. And we haven't seen a trace anywhere. I think he did it someplace else and just brought the head because it was easier that way."

Wager thought so, too, but that didn't answer why. "It's all got to be looked at."

"Yeah. What the hell, the pay's the same."

He wandered through the lanes of rose and lily beds toward a cluster of figures near a patio halfway across the open grounds. One or two roses still held flowers, but it was a last effort and the plants looked

29

weary and ready for winter; all but two or three lilies had bloomed and died, and the few remaining narrow leaves hung brown at the tip. He paused a moment: the browning of the long leaves, the flowerless lily stalks like a field of twigs, the weak sunlight finally burning away the overcast—all brought a memory of the tiger lilies that had filled every square inch of his aunt's yard that the kids hadn't worn flat with their running and games. Her house was no longer there— the whole neighborhood was no longer there, all of it scraped under and buried beneath brick-and-glass boxes. Urban renewal, they called it, though nothing had been renewed. It was just new. But here, among these lilies pulling life down into their roots, Wager again saw that house, those plants, smelled the cold darkness that wafted from under the wooden front porch and through the browning leaves of late-September mornings.

Memory. He tugged a brittle tip of a lily leaf and ground it to powder between thumb and forefinger. Maybe that was why the hair was combed and the head set like a bit of statue in the living green of the streamside: memory. And if that was it, then maybe she and her killer had been here before—or had somewhere shared some garden. Wager scooped a pinch of damp earth from the lily bed and sniffed its crisp cleanness. What kind of person? It was easy to shrug and answer, "Some nut." The evidence— Doyle's evidence—pointed at some nut. But in the back of his mind, Wager questioned if it was that simple.

The aggregate walk bent toward a small rectangle

of water that reflected mounds of sculpted earth rising like miniature Mayan temples. At first, he had not liked them because they were too angular to be natural. But as he wandered between their straight lines and open faces, they gave a sense that the flower beds were much, much larger; and they blocked the surrounding houses, streets, and apartments to create hollows of sky and privacy. At the highest part of the gardens, the main fountain gushed and splattered to fill the cool air with its sound. The water flowed through the grounds in lines and pools, ending at a final level near the patio where a knot of men gazed over a retaining wall at something on the west side. Wager went toward them.

Two uniformed officers glanced up. Wager identified himself to the corporal in charge. On the other side of the waist-high wall, two more officers dragged a grappling hook through a small, deep hole filled with scummy water and bordered by high weeds. Their shoes made sucking sounds as they moved.

"Nothing?" asked Wager.

"Not a goddamned thing. We'll be through here in a few minutes."

The final third of the grounds, weedy and unkept, sloped west toward the rusty gate and Cheesman Park across the street. On the garden's south edge, multi-windowed backs of mansions rose over a low hedge. Access could have been made there, but it was less likely; a person would have to cross private land, probably with a plastic bag in hand, past somebody's guard dogs or silent alarm system, and then scramble through the hedge. "Your people have gone along the tree line down there?"

"No trace of nothing."

Wager turned back toward the conservatory. In front of the main entrance, a group of senior citizens craned their necks. The lab people's cardboard sign "CRIME SCENE KEEP OUT" closed the admission window, and Wager heard an old woman's cracked voice ask over and over, "What? Why won't they let us in? What?"

Mr. Sumner, white hair now tamed, met him in the lobby. "We were supposed to open at nine, Inspector. We're an hour and fifty-one minutes past that. How much longer is this going on?"

"It shouldn't be much more. Did the medical examiner get here yet?"

"I really have no idea. The ambulance took the thing away, but there's still someone in the conservatory."

"Is Dominick Mauro here yet?"

Sumner gave a short, disgusted sigh and looked once more at the customers held outside the gate. "In Greenhouse One."

A lab man crouched to flip a fingerprint brush lightly at the outside handles of the emergency door. "Any luck?" asked Wager.

"Plenty—and all bad. When you get this many prints, you know none of them mean a thing."

"Nothing inside?"

"No. The alarm system for this door hasn't been tampered with, and there's no sign of forced entry anywhere. My guess is somebody used a key."

That was Wager's guess, too. He turned in to the

32

warm air of the first greenhouse; in the far corner, on folding chairs drawn up to a table with a large coffeepot and hot plate, sat three men. "Is Mr. Mauro here?"

"I'm him." The man closest to the pot stood. An inch or so taller than Wager and perhaps ten years older, Mauro had a thick round body that didn't show signs of softening. His nose had long ago been broken and moved slightly away from center.

"Detective Wager, homicide. Can I talk to you?"

"Why not?" He shoved a chair with his foot. "Sit down."

The other two men were unsure whether to go or stay. Then, without saying anything aloud, they decided it was their coffee break and Wager was the intruder. They sat and pretended not to hear his questions.

"Were you the last one to leave yesterday, Mr. Mauro?"

"No. It was my day off."

"On a Tuesday?"

"I worked last Sunday. Me and Sal change off weekends; whoever works Sunday gets next Tuesday off."

"Who locks up when you're not here?"

He bobbed his head at the two men in overalls. "Leon or Joe. They're the senior gardeners."

"They have keys, then?"

"Not their own. They use the emergency master—it's over there, locked in the keyboard."

A small steel cabinet with a glass door hung just inside the entry. It was secured by a combination padlock.

"It's that first key," added Mauro.

"They use the master to lock up the conservatory, then lock it in this greenhouse when they go home?"

"That's it."

"How many people know the combination to that padlock?"

"Only them, I guess. I don't know it, anyway."

"Can I talk to you two a minute?"

The elder of the two—lean, with large rimless bifocals—looked up. "Couldn't help hearing—me and Joe worked yesterday, but it was me that locked up. Leon Duncan is my name." He held out a hand that looked too wide for its thin wrist.

The second man stuck out his broad hand: "Joe Mazzotti. It's a terrible thing. Really terrible."

"Have you seen it?"

"Lord, no!" said Duncan. "We just heard about it when we come in to work."

Wager copied their names and addresses into his notebook. "Can you tell me what you did when you locked up last night, Mr. Duncan?"

"Sure I can. Mostly because there's not much to it. Nick, here, he's got the hard end of the job when it comes to locking up. Me, I just look through the conservatory and the bathrooms and lobby to make sure nobody's there. Then I lock up. We never had anybody get locked in yet; but if they did, they'd sure have a time getting out. No, no, wait. If they was in the conservatory itself, they could get out the emergency doors, but them bells would set off a racket."

"Yes, sir. Did you—?"

Duncan didn't hear him. "If they was in the lobby

section, now, they'd have the devil of a time, wouldn't they, Nick? All them doors is latched with a key and you can't open them without one, inside or out." Behind the bifocals, the eyes frowned. "But the telephone's in there, ain't it, Nick? They could always call somebody and get out that way. If they had a dime." Another pause. "I don't know what they'd do if they didn't have a dime."

The other groundskeeper nodded, and Wager got the feeling that was the most Mazzotti ever had a chance to do. "Yes, sir. Do you check out the other areas, too? Gift shop? Library?"

"No, I don't. Because those folks are supposed to shoo everybody out themselves, and I can't recollect ever finding their doors unlocked. I guess if I did, I'd look and see, though."

"What do you do after you lock the outside door?"

"After? Well, I put the key back in the cabinet and lock the greenhouse. Can't be too careful, what with them heads running around and everything."

"Yes, sir. Did anybody ever find the master key missing? Do you know if anybody ever lost one?"

"Well, I tell you—I been here almost eighteen years now, and the conservatory was built in 1966, that's ten years ago, and there ain't been no keys missing since then."

"How many people know the combination to that padlock?"

"Two. Me and Joe; that's all. That's all that needs to know. Anybody else wants a key to something, they can always find me or Joe."

Wager turned back to Mauro. "What's your routine

when you lock up?"

"I make sure the temperature and humidity's right in the conservatory; then I check the water timers and secure the conservatory doors. Then I check the education wing. Like Leon said, they're supposed to lock their own areas, but I check just in case; they've screwed up more than once over there. Then the thermostats in the lobby area . . . windows in the offices and gift shop. Then I mop the toilets and the lobby. Then I leave."

"See?" said Duncan. "He has a lot to do when he locks up."

"Yes, sir. Do you use the north doors, too, Mr. Mauro?"

"Yeah. There's only one set to lock."

"Do any of you know any females matching the victim's description—maybe twenty-five, short blond hair, regular features?"

"Do I know any?" answered Duncan. "Well, I see them around, you know, in the supermarket and such. But I sure don't know any."

Mauro and Mazzotti shook their heads.

"Could I have your address, Mr. Mauro, in case I have to get in touch with you again?"

"It's 1308 Garfield. Upstairs."

Upstairs. In that neighborhood, it meant a room or small apartment in a private home. "Do you live alone?"

"Yeah."

Wager wondered if his weariness made Mauro seem distant and almost sullen. God knew he was too tired now to come up with any more questions, and when he reached that stage the whole world seemed sullen. But at least by now his mind told him he had done enough, and he knew it would finally let him sleep. "Thanks a lot."

On his way back to the car, he glimpsed the lab technicians taking down the "CRIME SCENE" signs and saw the senior citizens finally line up at the admission window—and thought he heard a cracked female voice ask, "What? What do they want now?"

4

He came back on duty a bit before midnight. The two-tone brown office on the third floor was empty, as was the twenty-four-hour board that held bulletins, urgent messages from other shifts, replies to queries. No one from Wednesday's day or evening tours had questioned the apartment dwellers overlooking the Botanic Gardens. Or, if they had, there was nothing to report. Wager repeated the query for Ross and Devereaux, and added, "Let me know who you miss; I'll pick them up." He hoped that would gig Ross into not missing anyone.

From the top drawer of the filing cabinet, the one labeled "ACTIVE: CURRENT CASES UNSOLVED," Wager drew out the "Deceased Unknown" jacket with his initials on its lip. The folder held only a Xerox copy of the offense report filed by Officer Bauman; so far, the lab had come up with nothing. He read over both sides of the legal-sized sheet, especially the narrative section, but there was nothing that the policeman had omitted in talking to Wager. He telephoned the laboratory.

"Lab. Baird speaking."

"This is Wager. You people got anything yet on that head?"

"We have some photographs is all. The day shift took some impressions of the teeth and started the dental check, but you know how long that'll take. Besides, it hasn't been listed as a definite homicide."

The classification of death hadn't crossed his mind, but Baird was right—a homicide tag meant top priority and could save time. "Why not?"

"We don't know for sure how she died. There was nothing in the brain to indicate cause, and no marks on the skull. It's possible that it was natural causes."

"Jesus Christ—do you really think that?"

"Nope. But that's all the evidence says, Wager. The pathologist thinks the head was severed right after death, maybe within an hour. He'd have to see the rest of the body to be certain, but he can't declare the actual cause of death with what we have."

"Was a knife used?"

"It looks that way. The folds of skin indicate a cut made from behind and between the fifth and sixth cervical vertebrae, but the doc says that whoever did it sure as hell wasn't a surgeon."

"Why?"

"They tried to cut straight through instead of angling the blade. He found scratch marks on the lower tip of the fifth vertebra where the blade sawed before slipping between the bones. Apparently the victim was face down on a hard surface, and that compressed the vertebrae. Which makes sense—he wouldn't have to look her in the face while he hacked away."

"The doc thinks it was a man's arm?"

"A strong woman could do it. But most likely a man."

Wager jotted the information in his green notebook. "Could the doc get an idea of the time of death?"

"He needs the rest of the body to be certain."

Which no one had located since the head had been found this morning. His next call was to missing persons; after a dozen rings, a woman officer answered.

"This is Detective Wager in homicide. Has anybody reported a missing female, Anglo, around twenty-five, short blond hair?"

"Do you have a description of her clothing, sir?"

"No. All we got is the head." He was getting tired of saying that.

"What? Oh, yuk! Is that the one they found at the Botanic Gardens? I read about that in this afternoon's paper."

"Yes. The report probably came in during the last two or three days."

"Just a minute." It took her longer than Wager thought it should; she was probably covering four or five offices for the graveyard shift and didn't know the missing-persons layout. "Detective Wager? We have maybe a dozen reports on missing teen-aged girls in the last week, and three for elderly women. But nothing in that age group."

"If anything comes in, would you let me know?"

"Yes sir. I'll put it in the request file."

And that, he thought, would be the last anyone ever heard of his request. He drained a cup of coffee from the machine in the hall and then headed for the records section. Chances were against him on this, but it was a thread and, like all the others, had to be tugged. A tall brunette, whose starched blue police shirt swelled out nicely, smiled at him. Wager filled request slips for Solano, Duncan, Mauro, Mazzotti, and

Sumner, and pushed them with his I.D. card across the small shelf toward the hovering breasts that bore the chrome name tag, "J. Fabrizio."

"Just a minute, please."

Beneath the dark uniform skirt, her slender legs slowly unveiled as she leaned further and further over the open trays of records. From around the large center block of pillars and wiring boards that was the communications center of records strolled a tall uniformed cop, another one whose blond curly hair looked too long for Wager's liking. He said something to J. Fabrizio, his voice lost in the clatter and humming of teletypes, police frequencies, typewriters, and the inevitable radio music; but the hand he placed on the curve of her hip spoke more than words. She pulled straight, the profile of her mouth saying "not here."

"We don't have anything on most of these, Detective Wager. Here's an old file on Mauro, Dominick Steven. It's the only Dominick Mauro we have. We can put the others on LETS, if it's real important."

That was the Law Enforcement Teletype System used to request information from police agencies all over the country. But there was no sense wasting time looking somewhere else for people who had lived in Denver most of their lives. As for Mauro, Wager stared at the old-style folder with its black-and-white photograph and realized now that he'd half expected a jacket on the man. It had not been just the weariness that made Wager think Mauro was keeping his distance. "Let me have this one."

"Yes sir. If you'll just initial here."

He signed out the file and took it to one of the narrow reading shelves. It was a thin folder, the last entry dated some twenty years ago. Mostly kid crap and hotheaded stuff: stolen car, assault (dismissed), disturbing the peace, assault (conviction); time served—seven months at Buena Vista reformatory. Nothing after that. The parole officer's reports were favorable, and his last entry cleared the file. It wasn't much, but it was a record; and Wager, like most cops, knew that a record meant a troublemaker.

Just beyond the entry to records was the contact card file, a large gray machine that cranked four-foot bins in alphabetical order past the viewer. He pushed the advance button until the revolving tray labeled "M-N-O" swung down. Then he thumbed through the "Ma——" listings twice. None of the white cards bore Mauro's name; for the past five years, no cop had any reason to remember him.

Sitting once more at the wooden desk that must have been military surplus—it was like so many of those he had seen in various company headquarters during his eight years in the Marine Corps—he leafed through the pages of his small notebook as the same questions came up again and again. Why just the head? How did the killer get a key? Who was the victim? Maybe when they found out who she was, he'd get answers. But on the midnight-to-eight shift, no office was open for him to hassle into moving a little faster.

He drew off another cup of coffee and sat down again to think. Entry to the conservatory—that had to be with a key. And whoever did it was telling some-

body something—himself, the victim, the world—
something. Wager closed his eyes to recall the paths
and plants and sculpted earth and stream inside the
long building. There were maybe three other grottoes
like the one where the head was found: a moss area
against the wall near the delivery door, the fern-
draped wishing pond across from the mosses, and,
halfway up the conservatory, a little bridge fringed
with bamboo. But the largest and prettiest and most
private corner was where it had been set. Whoever
had done it knew his way around the conservatory,
and he had done it with care: the place was visible
only from the short path across the stream; he had
placed it in a frame of living plants. With his eyes still
closed, Wager could almost see a man—he kept thinking of the person as a man—carefully step from the
main path and lean far down the forward slope of the
steep bank above the stream, gently prop the head
beneath the soft green of one of the room's largest
plants, and then carefully comb its hair. Next,
flashlight in hand, the man had crumbled the earth
packed by the weight of his feet and dragged it
smooth with his palm. Then—and Wager would have
sworn to this—he went around and up the short path
on the other side of the stream to look at the head. He
probably shined the flashlight on it; the foundation
was shoulder-high at that point, so he wouldn't be
afraid of being seen from outside the glass walls. If he
went to so much trouble to place the head, to comb
the hair, then he wanted to admire his work. There
he stood or squatted—he could see better if he
squatted—for how long? With eyes closed, Wager

could almost touch the figure in his mind: a man squatting silhouetted from the back by the dim glow of a flashlight, the beam catching here and there on jutting leaves that glowed translucent and still and formed a ragged shadow to surround the small circle of light thrown against the far bank. And in the center of that bright circle, white against the black earth, the head gapped silently back at the crouching man. Saying what? And what did he say to the head? For Wager knew that, too: they had talked to each other.

The telephone's rattle jarred him from his thoughts and it took a moment to understand the male voice on the other end of the line. "Who?"

"Gargan—with the *Post!* Come on, Wager, you know who I am!"

He knew the police reporter, all right. "I didn't hear you the first time."

"I thought maybe you didn't want to talk to your old buddy." Gargan's voice said he still thought that.

"Not so," lied Wager. "It's always nice."

"Yeah—I know how you love us hard-working reporters. Listen, I'm told you're the officer in charge on that head found out at the Botanic Gardens this morning—yesterday morning, now. You got anything more on it?"

"We haven't been able to identify the victim yet."

"What's taking so long?"

"We don't have a large body of information, Gargan."

"Oh, that's sick, Wager. That isn't even funny."

"I didn't mean it to be funny!"

44

"Yeah . . . I think I really do believe you. How about letting me know when you get something? The story's been picked up by the wire services and they want a follow-up."

"Check with the public information officer in the morning."

"You people don't have a public information officer! It's just you and me, baby, and a wire-service story."

"Gargan, maybe I'm new in this division, but I damn well know we don't have favorite reporters. You call me, and if I have something, I'll let you know. Just like I will any other reporter. I'm sure as hell not going to take time to call you, because I've got too goddamned much work to do." He started to hang up.

"Hey! Wager!"

"What?"

"Being on the narc squad makes people a little flaky, you know? I sure hope you got your transfer in time. But I doubt it."

Wager hung up; *perro que no muerde, ladra*—a dog barks when he can't bite. In that saying, he heard his mother's voice smoothing away the taunts and gibes from neighborhood kids who had called him a coyote—a half-breed. And here he was still a half-breed—half cop, half something else, even in the eyes of other cops. Still yapped at by shitbirds like Gargan. He belched loudly from the warm fumes of the coffee; he'd like to tell Gargan and every other reporter to stick it, but Doyle's procedure manual said the taxpayers had a right to know and that officers would cooperate with the press wherever possible. Fine. But, like Ross, Gargan would have to keep up if he could.

Wager closed the little notebook and returned the Jane Doe folder to the active drawer. Then he holstered his radio pack and finished the coffee. It was time to be on the street, time to put in his eight hours as backup for the uniformed officers. He had specific areas of the city to cruise: Five Points, various housing projects, the Curtis Park region, East Colfax. That was where most of the trouble would be found, and if he was on the scene, he could prevent a hell of a lot instead of having to sweep up the shit afterward. And on the midnight-to-eight shift, routine patrol was most of the job—which was why Doyle had put him on it to start with. In a way, it was like slipping on a pair of old, comfortable shoes that had been lost in the closet for a long time. It was like strolling an old beat after years away from it: some things were changed on the surface—buildings, faces, names— but underneath it still felt the same because it was the same. Wager slipped into it with the comfortable feeling of coming home.

5

It took three more days, until Sunday night, before Wager found a copy of an offense report bearing his name in red pencil waiting for him on the twenty-four-hour board. The top line, "Event," was homicide; the square for marking "Original Report" had been scratched over and a new check put in the square for "Additional Report," with Wager's initials printed beneath in the same red pencil. He skipped past the other information sections marked off by alternating pale blue and white panels to "Narrative." There was, of course, no statement from the victim; the witness, twelve-year-old Rubio Valdez, reported finding a body wrapped in a large plastic garbage bag and stuffed in the trunk of a junked car at a wrecking lot at above address. Witness said he and other kids were playing in cars at junkyard, and he pulled out the back seat of said vehicle and saw through a hole in the trunk paneling a bundle of some kind. Witness then pried open trunk lid and found heavy black plastic bag that smelled bad. Peeked inside and saw knees. Witness ran home and mother called police. Reporting officer arrived at scene and discovered an Anglo female, age unknown, nude, missing head. She appeared to be dead. Called homicide. Detectives Ross and Devereaux responded with medical examiner at 15:00 hours.

Wager went back to the top of the form and began

taking notes. Officer Ronald Pearce had received the complaint at 14:42, 24 October '76; details at time of offense unknown. Victim, white female, Jane Doe, age undetermined, no suspects, no witnesses to crime. Found in disabled vehicle: 1968 Buick sedan, no plates. Reporting officer looked in bag to examine contents. Victim apparently dead for several days. Cause of death unknown.

On a piece of paper clipped behind the offense report was a note in red pencil: "Wager—no info from lab yet (16:45). But unless we got an epidemic of sloppy barbers, this one's all yours. Ross. P.S. List of apartments near Botanic Gardens in case file."

Wager lifted the file from the drawer and began reading the legal-sized sheet of addresses as he dialed the number of the police laboratory.

"Lab. Baird speaking."

"This is Wager. Do you have a match-up on that torso and head?"

"We can't go into court with it, but it looks pretty sure. The blood type's the same, type A; and as far as we can tell from what hasn't decayed, the edges of the neck and torso fit. Right at the fifth vertebra. But we sent the skin samples over to Denver General's lab to run the tissue tests. We're not set up to do that here."

"Who'd you send it to?"

"Dr. Jaffe. She's about the best tissue specialist we can get. But don't go bugging her, Gabe—she likes to give the information direct to us, instead of having a lot of different police officers calling for it."

"When's she going to have something?"

"It got there on a weekend, Detective Wager. Not

48

everybody works twenty-four hours a day, seven days a week. She'll get to it sometime tomorrow, and we'll let you know just as soon as her report comes back. And before you ask, Gabe: right, we are trying to identify the torso; no, we don't have anything on the dental work; and right, we do have a set of pictures if you want them."

"I'll be right down."

"I wouldn't be too eager."

He hung up and finished studying the list of apartment and condominium numbers that Ross and Devereaux had finally managed to interview on their shift. That was another problem of the midnight-to-eight tour: any follow-up work had to be either on your own time, which was all right if you had it, or on somebody else's time, which was never all right. But people working normal hours didn't take kindly to answering questions after ten at night. In fact, as Wager scanned the long list of addresses, each with its "X," meaning no information, or "O," meaning no one home to respond, he wondered if it was really worth going back to visit all the "O"s—the trespass into the conservatory must have taken place so late that most of the people were asleep. But he folded the sheet into his coat pocket anyway, knowing that he would go back over the list for those not questioned. If he didn't, his mind would itch.

He tried missing persons one more time; after a long series of rings, the same female voice, less friendly, answered the question he once more asked her: "No, Detective Wager, we still have no requests answering that description."

Fred Baird was at his small desk fiddling with a rack of four test tubes when Wager came in. He glanced up and pulled a handful of photographs from a file separator. "Any civilians you show these to better have a strong stomach."

This far from the communications center and the duty watch, no sound of police frequencies or country-and-Western music echoed in the corridors, and the silence of the labs was made deeper by the hum of fluorescent lights in the ceiling. Wager spread the 5" × 7" color photographs along the cool metal of the laboratory bench. The first ones were from the Botanic Gardens, and the glare of the flash bulb made the head's yellow-white face lean forward out of the dark earth. The bloodstains on dirt and skin stood out more starkly in the photograph than they had in the conservatory, and Wager noticed for the first time the faint line of pancake make-up spread like a thin mask from just below the hair to under the curve of the loose jaw. The bloodless neck was white above its fringe of sagging, empty skin, and in the hard light the creases in the neck looked like lines inked on the flesh. The next pictures were the morgue shots. An attendant tilted the head back on an empty slab so the severed neck could be seen clearly; the identification slate in the foreground was chalked with "Jane Doe, 20 Oct. '76, F.B." The initials stood for Fred Baird. If necessary, the photographer could be called upon in court to testify that he had taken the picture and that the object in the picture was in fact the evidence he'd seen with his own eyes.

The photographs of the torso began with general

surveys of the junkyard and then moved to the car and the open trunk. After the series of photographs that showed the scene as discovered, a series depicted the victim being unwrapped for identification at the scene. Ross stood beside the open trunk of a rusty dark blue Buick, holding open the black plastic bag in which a pale glimmer showed. Other shots followed each stage of the body's removal and had a detective or the medical examiner facing the camera to establish a witness at the scene.

"I guess you didn't find any prints or traces in the area?" Otherwise Ross would have pushed the results as far as possible, trying to solve the case before Wager could reclaim it.

"I wasn't on duty, but here's a copy of the lab search findings—nothing."

The sheet of paper Baird handed him was brief, the entry in most sections a terse "negative." The remarks space noted, "Heavy rain the night of 23 Oct. Soil and paint chip samples taken. Case number 17815462."

Wager leafed slowly through the pictures once more, looking not so much at the car or the body, but at the bits and pieces of blurred background—a junkyard littered with weeds, trash, rusting car bodies. Bodies. Tossed away like junk. But not the head. That had been placed very carefully. "There's got to be something there."

Wager had spoken to himself, but Baird misunderstood. "If you get a suspect, and if the suspect doesn't clean his shoes, and if we can find those shoes, then we may have a link through soil sample. That's about the best we've got."

"None of it's worth a damn without a suspect." Wager turned to the morgue pictures of the nude torso. These offered different angles of the body on the open plastic garbage bag. In a few, an attendant propped it up as it had been found. The remainder were of the torso straightened as much as possible on a morgue slab and washed of the thick smears of old blood in order to reveal any wounds and identifying marks or scars. Maroon patches of flesh like massive birthmarks showed where the blood had settled as she lay wadded up. In one shot, the morgue attendant pointed to the severed neck; in another, to the chest just below the left breast where a one-inch puncture wound swelled black and taut with decay. Wager looked closely at the wrists and arms, but no marks of violence were visible. The photographer's initials on the I.D. slate were "L.W.J."

"Who's L.W.J?"

"Lincoln W. Jones. He's on the afternoon shift this month."

"What's the doc say?"

"He hasn't had time for the complete autopsy—he's doing it now. So far, it looks like she was dead for twelve to sixteen hours before being put in the car. You can see lividity here on the hip points and breasts—that's the marks from blood settling before she was moved for the last time. The rigor of these joints here and here was broken in order to stuff her into the bag." He looked up to explain to the new man in homicide: "Once the rigor's broken, a joint won't stiffen up again."

"How long was it in the first position before it was moved?"

"Can't say for sure—it depends on characteristics of the body as well as temperature and so on. The guess is eight to twelve hours. Then she was transported to the junkyard. The darkest marks along the upper back and here, in the hands and forearms, came after she was positioned in the car's trunk."

"Could the marks be bruises?" Wager asked.

"No tissue damage. It's lividity."

"So that stab wound is the probable cause of death?"

"The pathologist wants to finish running tests on the fluids and organs before he says for certain. But it looks to me like it was."

"Why?"

"Well, the lividity marks indicate that a lot of blood was left in the body—I figure that means the heart stopped pumping before the neck artery was opened. That's a heart wound there. But of course I'm just a flunky, not the expert."

"Any signs of sexual assault?"

"The doc'll let you know in good time, Wager. Denver's a small town—we go at a slow pace. And we all want to live long enough to collect our pensions." Baird poured himself a cup of coffee from a beaker steaming over a Bunsen burner. "Do you know that stress-related diseases are the number-one cop killer? Your life expectancy, Mr. Cop, is fifty-seven years."

"The Motor Vehicle Division has no prints for her?"

"If they did, we'd have an I.D. by now, wouldn't we?"

He was halfway back to his office with the duplicate set of pictures when the radio pack called his number.

"This is X-eighty-five." The detective division's prefix was "X"; the 800 series meant homicide. Wager was detective number 5.

"You got somebody to see you in your office. What's your ten-twenty?"

"I'm in the building. I'm on my way."

"Ten-four."

It was Gargan, in the same black turtleneck that he always wore. Wager occasionally wondered if that was its original color or if it had soiled that way. Now the reporter was trying to grow a moustache that framed his mouth in a horseshoe of bristling orange hair which had snagged a crumb or two of his supper. "Gabe! Lay it on me, man—what's new on the horseless headsman?"

"Here. Get a laugh out of this." He tossed the pictures on the desk.

"Oh, Jesus." The reporter's face twisted, and he pushed them back at Wager. "The wire services can't use these. How about names or numbers? Got an I.D. yet?"

"No. All I can say is that it looks like the head and the torso go together, but you better wait for a complete report from the pathologist before quoting that."

"Was the—ah—severing the cause of death?"

"The lab doesn't think so. The doc said it was a sloppy job, and there's no indication on the torso that the hands were tied. Nobody would just stand there and let some guy saw at their neck."

54

"What's this he's pointing to, a stab wound?"

"Yes. But it might not be the cause of death. We'll know more when the doc files his report."

"Jesus. Whoever did it must be totally bug-fuck."

"Or maybe wants us to think so."

"Yeah. Believe me, I think so." Gargan slapped his feet from the rung of a neighboring chair. "And of course you don't have any suspects?"

"We don't even have any witnesses, Gargan. But we *are* working on the case."

"Denver's citizenry can sleep better for knowing that." He stood by a bulletin board and tapped the pen-and-ink composite of a face on a circular from New Mexico describing the suspect in an Indian turquoise robbery and murder. "This looks like my brother-in-law. And I wouldn't put it past the bastard to do something like that. Except he'd get caught sooner." The reporter paused in the doorway. "Well, I'll just have to say that you think the head and body are the same person, but you're waiting verification from the lab."

"That's about it."

"I'd appreciate hearing if you get something—don't forget, we're old buddies, Gabe."

"Right." He stayed at his desk until Gargan had time to clear the police building; then he went on the street to put in another eight hours.

6

Monday brought one of those afternoons that made Wager's small apartment feel empty no matter how much he prowled it. He straightened the NCO's sword he'd hung on a wall and the two sling chairs he seldom used and the small photograph of a single dead tree that was a souvenir from an earlier case. Strange how the restless emptiness came most often when a lot of work was going for nothing—and how it seemed even stronger now that he was in homicide. Maybe because in narcotics there had been no clear victims, only scum everywhere—users who turned pushers when they had enough to sell, buyers who bought because they had to, pushers who worked for you or against you depending on the money. But homicide had a victim who lay there waiting for an answer and whose silence was an accusation against Wager.

He flipped the television set from one channel of squealing contestants to another and then snapped it off and padded barefoot into the kitchen to begin chopping onion for a small breakfast steak. Despite years of rotating day and night shifts, he had never adapted to a combination of eggs and late-afternoon sun.

And, as usual, the apartment's faint echo made him think of Lorraine. Which was silly, because the victim didn't look anything like Lorraine. His ex-wife's hair was reddish brown and long, and turned gold only when she fanned it smoothly over her shoulders in the sun. He wondered if it was still that way, if she still wore it straight down her back. And he wondered why he bothered wondering; two years was a long time, and even then he had not often seen her hair spread in the sun like that. *Una mujer sabrosa.* That's what he called her—a savory woman. And she had been. But she was not a cop's wife.

On his last visit to his mother's, his sister had been sure to tell him—using the voice that went all the way back to the smell of chalk dust and oiled schoolroom halls, to the pervasive rotting-apple-and-wet-paper-bag smell of third grade—that Lorraine now had a boyfriend. Who was not a cop.

"What's he do?" Wager couldn't help the question.

"What business is it of yours?"

It wasn't, any more. But what business did his sister have to say anything in the first place? Not that it ever stopped her. "It's a cop's question. I'm a cop."

"You sure are."

The rest of the dinner had been very strained.

He poured himself another cup of coffee and wandered out on his apartment's small balcony thrust over Downing Street ten floors below. Behind Denver, the tops of the shadowed mountains merged with piles of cloud pushing in from Utah to make the peaks seem even taller, even darker. Above the heavy cloud banks, an orange streak of contrail caught the sun as an airplane left Stapleton International for San Francisco or Los Angeles. Wager had been to California once. Camp Pendleton. He remembered the hills lying tawny and empty to a steady wind; and the ocean, even emptier, which moved and writhed wherever his eye rested, and which, despite its name, was never peaceful. Maybe he would take a vacation someday and see more of California. God knows he had the time coming. He drained his coffee and padded back to the kitchen to rinse the cup out. Crap on a vacation. He didn't really want one. He didn't know anybody in California. What he really wanted was the victim's name. There wasn't one more goddamned thing he could do until he knew her name, and the longer that took, the longer the odds were against a conviction.

He dressed and glanced over the items in his small green notebook, deciding to put off the telephone work until later and to do the legwork while it was still light. His first stop was the area where the torso had been found the previous afternoon. It took him awhile to twist his way over the rough streets and bumpy railroad tracks between grimy columns that lifted the bed of the Valley Freeway above this part of Denver. The old factories and foundries lining the railroad spurs were closed for the day, and the empty remnants of buildings that had been condemned long ago but never torn down were boarded shut with faded plywood or rotten beams. He finally passed the tangle of weeds and willow and stretches of wet sand that was the shallow South Platte River, and turned in to a short street of sagging buildings. Here and there, sprayed graffiti spelled gang names; Wager remembered "Los Lobos" from ten years past. The "Iron Men" had been even before his time. There were no new names. In a small turret capping the second floor of a deserted office building, a square stone held the date 1892. He stopped in the middle of the empty street to listen. Behind, from the Valley Highway on the other side of the South Platte, came the roar of heavy traffic; in front, but out of sight behind a tree-less embankment, were the hiss and blat of Federal Avenue, with its neon and glass, its chrome gas stations, its street lights, its drive-in banks. But here, in this short lane of deserted buildings, inert trash, and black, glassless windows, was nothing. Not a voice, not a flower, not even a stray cat. It was one of the few corners of Denver that seemed, to Wager, absolutely dead. And at the far end of the silent street was the junkyard.

Sprawling over half a block and across to the Federal Avenue embankment, the crumpled and rusting cars washed up against a sagging chain-link fence and around the rotting walls of a lone house that served as an office. A single bulb burned whitely over the closed front door where the porch had been ripped away to leave a pale A-shaped scar like a startled eyebrow. Not even a junkyard dog answered when Wager called through the locked and rusted gate. He crossed the brick street to the pile of twisted cars and trucks tossed into the weeds. The dark Buick, one of those round bulging models, sat in an unfenced portion of the lot a short dozen paces from the curb. Wager gazed at it, at the empty buildings. Not far south rose the belching smokestacks of the power company's downtown plant; if he stood on the Buick's fender, he could just glimpse the access road that tied this forgotten corner with Federal Avenue. North, but hidden behind the Colfax viaduct, were the basketball arena and Mile-High Stadium. If a person knew which twists of road to follow, he could get here from the stadium's parking lots. Otherwise it was damned hard to find. Yet someone—in the dark and without much fumbling around—had found it. Somebody had parked close to the Buick, knowing where in the lightless street to stop; he had lifted an awkward body in a slippery plastic bag and carried it to the trunk that he knew would be unlocked. Slammed the lid; maybe cleaned up a bit in the night, even dragged the clay patches that cracked here and there among the weed clumps to smear the trace of his footprints. And had left.

A dead corner that the city had thrown away, stripped and broken cars rusting away in the brown weeds. Wager knew this spot had not been picked by accident. The head was set in a living place, the lifeless body tossed aside with other worthless junk.

Wager could feel that as clearly as he felt the points of shattered bottles beneath his shoes. But to know it didn't answer why. Or who.

He spent the next four hours visiting the apartments near the Botanic Gardens, knocking at the list of numbers bearing Ross's "O" that said no one answered the first time. Like Ross and Devereaux, Wager didn't bother with units above the fifth floor; at that distance in the dark, no one could have seen anything anyway. And, like Ross and Devereaux, he got negative answers. The routine was pretty much the same at each door: a sudden blotting of the tiny light in the peephole after Wager knocked, and a muffled "Yes?"

"Detective Wager," holding his shield up to the peephole. "I'm investigating a death on some property behind the apartments. Can I ask you a question or two?"

A moment of startled silence, then the door opening to the end of its safety chain to show half a face. "Who?"

"Detective Wager. Denver Police. Did you happen to notice anything at all unusual taking place in the Botanic Gardens during the night of Tuesday October 19th?"

"No! We keep our curtains closed at night."

"Thank you." And on to the next "O".

It was nearing ten. The women who now answered had faces scoured of make-up and the men wore sport-shirts with little alligators on the front or shiny robes tied over their pajamas. Wager moved to the last apartment on the fourth floor. There the answer was different.

"That was last Tuesday, you say?"

"Yes, sir."

"You know, I did see something weird. I kind of wondered about it at the time."

"You did? What?"

The man's half-face in the doorway was thin, with dark, bushy eyebrows that lifted as they approached each other. At first, Wager thought the man was puzzled; then he realized that the eyebrows stayed that way. "A light. But not like they have sometimes. A flashlight, maybe. I couldn't sleep, and went out on the balcony for some air. I saw this light moving around in the conservatory. Our balcony looks almost right down on it."

"Can I come in? Can I see this balcony?"

"I guess." The chain slipped to let him into a narrow living room. The man said, "Just a minute," and shut a side door. "The wife's in bed."

"Is this it?" The far end of the living room was a panel of orange-and-blue drapes that seemed to go either with or against the square, glossy white sofa and low glass-and-chrome table. Wager wasn't quite sure which.

"Yes." The man pulled open the drapes and rolled back the thick glass door. The balcony was wide enough for two folding chairs and a small charcoal grill; over the lip of its wire-and-wood panel, the grounds of the Botanic Gardens were a large, dark hole surrounded by city lights and the swirl of traffic.

"Right down there's the conservatory."

The diamond-shaped faces of its roof glinted in the dark, and from the far end, toward the lobby section, a purple glow shone fuzzily. That would be the moss section; apparently the fluorescent wands were on all night. At this end, where the head was found, all was dark.

"Can I have your name, sir?"

"What for?"

"It's just routine. Any information I get, I'm supposed to have a name for."

"Mikkelson. Ronald Mikkelson."

"Want to tell me what you saw, Mr. Mikkelson?"

"Like I said, I came out for some air and was leaning on the railing right where you are, and I happened to look down. . . . No, wait a minute—something caught my eye. That was it—there was a flash right down there, and it caught my eye, and through the roof of the conservatory I saw this dot of light. It was a flashlight, I'm sure of it."

"Did it do anything?"

"Let's see. . . . It moved around a little and then got dim. Then it was still for a real long time, like it was propped somewhere. Then it moved again and went out."

"Did you see anybody in the light?"

"No. You can't really see through the glass—it's tinted or something. You can see lights on the other side, but you can't see much detail."

"About how long would you say the light was on?"

"Ten minutes. Long enough for me to start getting cold."

"How long were you out here before you saw the flash of light?"

"I'm not sure. Maybe five minutes."

"Did you hear anything before the light came on?"

"Like what?"

"A car. A door. Somebody walking in the alley."

"There's always cars." He thought hard. "No—I really can't say I heard anything."

"Have you ever seen anything like that before?"

"Not just like that, no. Sometimes they have the lights on at night for working or when they've got a bunch of people coming in for something or other. But this was different."

"Did you think about telling the police what you saw?"

"No. I didn't make much of it at the time. Do you really think it was somebody putting that head there?"

Somebody with a key that fit silently into locks, somebody with a flashlight who crouched and stared. "It could be."

"I didn't hear about it until yesterday. I saw it on the news last night—they said you guys found the rest of her in a car over on the west side."

"Yes, sir. About what time did you see this light?"

"Two. Maybe two-thirty in the morning. Can we go back in now? It's getting chilly." He rolled the balcony door shut and pulled the drapes across the glass.

"Did you notice any people in the area?"

"No. It's too dark to see anything in the alley."

Wager was finishing his notes when the bedroom door clicked softly open to show a blinking, frowning woman pulling a feathery dressing gown over her shoulders. "Ron? Who is this? What's going on?"

"He's a detective from the police."

"Police! My God—what's happened? What's he want with you, Ron?"

"Me? Nothing! He was asking about the lights I saw in the conservatory. Remember? I told you about them last night."

She pushed a string of hair up under the pink ruffle of a plastic nightcap and blinked again. "That's all? You're sure that's all?"

"What else do you think it would be?"

"Good night, Mr. Mikkelson. Ma'am."

Neither answered Wager.

"Well, how would you like to wake up and find a policeman in our own living room talking to me?" she asked.

"I'd sure as hell ask why, Sherri, before jumping to conclusions!"

Wager closed the apartment door behind him, dimming Mikkelson's rising voice: "And just what the hell did you think I . . ."

He reported for the Tuesday shift the usual fifteen minutes before midnight. Ross and Devereaux were wrapping up an investigation of discharge of firearms by an officer on duty. It was another of homicide's jobs to investigate every bullet fired by an officer whether or not injury resulted.

"Here he comes, leaping tall buildings with a single fart." Ross thumped a date stamp on a document. "If you come in any earlier, Wager, me and Dev can stay at home."

"It's my time."

"Yeah. There's a note for you from the lab. They said to call." He gestured at the twenty-four-hour board. "Are you still running around on that mutilation death?"

"And not getting anywhere. We don't have any identification yet."

"You'd be better off waiting for that. In the five years I've been doing this shit, most cases solve themselves once the victim's family and friends are known."

"Ross is right," said Devereaux. He pointed to a long, detailed chart covering a quarter of one wall. It broke down ten years of homicides into statistics matching the F.B.I.'s Uniform Crime Report. "The pattern's changing, but most of the killings are still the result of a little excess emotion by friends or loved ones. The stranger-to-stranger stuff comes as part of another crime—rape, robbery, maybe a professional hit. And maybe you just got a loony with this one. Anybody who'd do that must be nuts. But when they come in cold and without witnesses, there's no sense busting your balls until the victim's identified."

That might be all right if someone other than the killer knew she was dead. But so far, it seemed no one even knew she'd ever been alive. "I don't like sitting on my tail."

Ross snorted and shoved his papers into an interoffice mailing envelope and whipped the short string around the cardboard button. "No cop does, Wager. You're not so special."

"I don't claim to be. But it's my way of working. If it's no good, I'll hear it from the chief."

"You sure will." Ross left.

Wager telephoned the police lab. "Baird? This is Wager. I got a note to call you."

The voice on the other end of the line said, "Hang on," followed by a muffled clatter as the receiver was set down. Then, "The coffee was boiling over; these beakers aren't worth a damn for making coffee in."

"What do you have for me, Fred?"

"A couple of things. The tissue and blood tests have come back—the head and torso belong together. No question. But the coroner's report on the torso isn't so good."

"What's that mean?"

"It's not as conclusive as we'd like—the trunk of that car got hot in the sun, and the plastic bag kept all the moisture in, so the decomposition and the generation of gases and bacteria was accelerated. It's hard to be conclusive about what she ate. The guess is this: her stomach seemed nearly empty—maybe some fruit and cheese, but again that's just a guess. The blood showed a trace of alcohol, but we can't tell how much. No clear indication of narcotics or poisons anywhere in the system, but they could be there. It comes to damn little that can stand up in court."

Wager jotted it down anyway. "Could the doc tell how long after death the head was severed?"

"That's guesswork, too. Maybe an hour."

"Was the stab wound the primary cause of death?"

"It's the only clear cause. But because of the decomposition of the organs, some son of a bitch might challenge it in court." His voice grew almost happy as he moved to more definite facts. "The wound was in good condition, though—it measures three centimeters wide, eleven deep. The shape of the perforation indicates a single-edged knife; all in all, it looks like a butcher knife. A single thrust entered between the third and fourth ribs at approximately fifteen degrees below horizontal plane and thirty degrees left of the sagittal plane. What that means is—"

"That the killer was right-handed."

A moment of silence. "Right, Wager! That's pretty good!"

He wondered why the specialists always thought they were the only ones who could read technical manuals. "What damage did it do?"

"Oh—it penetrated the left ventricle and severed the aorta and partly severed the pulmonary artery. It was a good thrust—death was instantaneous. There was also a contained haemopericardium tamponade. Guess what that means, you bastard."

"Just tell me, Baird."

"It means the blood didn't come out of the wound but stayed in the cavity around the heart. Say, did you know that most people are right-handed and have hearts on the left side? God made it that way so people could stab each other easier."

No, Wager did not know that; and he didn't give a damn for jokes made to show how tough a person was. "Did the doc check her fingernails?"

"Right. Very clean. No flesh or hair. Heavily painted and carefully manicured. Looks like professional care."

"Anything else?"

"Right. We ran an adhesive test on the stab wound and came up with what looks like bits of fiber. It looks like the knife cut through cloth before entering the body; we sent the samples on to the F.B.I. lab for identification."

"Any evidence of sex?"

"Other than the body being stripped, nothing. No tissue damage or indication of sperm traces in vagina, anus, or mouth. That's about the only examination the condition of the body would allow. Hell, if the killer's a crock, he probably wouldn't screw her anyway—he'd cream his pants when he killed her."

"Yeah. Send me a full copy of the report when

you can."

"Right."

He poured himself a mug of coffee and stared at the file, the notes, the envelope that held the photographs. A killer stood close enough to make a single thrust with a wide blade. No struggle—no scratching that left traces under the victim's fingernails, no bruises on the head or body from a preliminary assault. No evidence of sexual relations. And no one yet asking missing persons for her—not even a week later. All right, let's look at it this way: she's drinking a little booze, and the killer steps right in front of her to stab her without a struggle—it all points to somebody she knew. To some place she felt comfortable in. Time sequence? The coroner's evidence puts the body in two positions—face down just after death while the head's cut off; then, twelve to sixteen hours later, doubled up in the trunk of the Buick. Of course that was a guess. Hell, everything was a guess; Wager could guess, too. According to the witness Mikkelson, the head could have been put in the conservatory around 2 A.M. Wager counted hours on his fingers back from 2 A.M. Twelve to sixteen hours back—give or take the time he would need to go from the junkyard to the conservatory or vice versa. Between, say, 10 A.M. on Tuesday, October 19th, and 2 A.M. on Wednesday, October 20th. Wager printed the times and date in block letters on a separate page of the little book and absently etched lines around it. The suspect would need an alibi for that time. And a key. That damned key. The victim knew someone who had a key. And a place. Wherever the killing and cutting took place, there would be a hell of a lot of blood. A place to leave the body stretched out until it was bagged and toted to the junkyard. An assault without a struggle, a little butchering without interruption, time to clean up, then transporting the victim at night, and no one asking for her. Hell, Wager almost smiled at himself for wasting time: it added up to a whore making a house call in an apartment with a bathtub. And there were only half a million such places in the city. But the living green and the dead junk; head in one, body in the other. That, too, was a key—and a puzzle.

Still, without a witness, without knowing the victim's name, Wager felt his mind sketch in things about the killer. But slowly, slowly; *"Quien anda al revés, anda el camino dos veces."* He could still hear his grandfather warning him when he was anxious and bouncing to be turned loose on some half-baked project, and was answering, "Yes, sir; yes, sir, I understand," and not hearing a word of the instructions. Wager had long since learned that it was no pleasure to walk the same road twice.

And he did feel something solid forming from the web of his thoughts.

The telephone's ring pulled him back to the brown box of the homicide office. Gargan was asking what else had been found.

"The tissue test matches the head and torso," answered Wager.

"Any identification of the victim?"

"Nothing yet."

"Anything in the coroner's report about dope or sex?"

"The body was too decayed to be conclusive."

"Thanks heaps."

"Anytime," Wager said.

After he got rid of Gargan, he tried missing persons again. That was something that bothered him as much as the key—no one seemed to know that the person was missing.

"We haven't had any listing like her, Detective Wager. I really will call you as soon as we do." The female voice clicked off.

Thanks heaps to you, too. Wager felt a sour grin in the back of his mind: a bad word always comes back. He drained his almost cold coffee and scraped the papers and envelopes into the manila cover of the Jane Doe file. Maybe Ross and Devereaux were right; maybe it was better just to let the case wait and start working it when the identification came in. If it came in. Maybe. But Wager knew that he had something more than air in his hands. He couldn't yet call it a profile of the killer, but he did sense something about the suspect's mind.

He slammed shut the file drawer and was pulling on his jacket when the telephone called him back to his desk. It was Baird.

"The dental records just came through—we got an identification!"

"Let's have it."

"Rebecca Jean Crowell. She had a lot of orthodontist work done in . . . let's see, 1973 to 1974. The dentist is a local one . . . Albert Miller. His office is down near the Cherry Creek shopping center, 105 Milwaukee Street."

"Any address for the victim?"

"As of May, 1974, she listed 2418 Tremont, Apartment 3. No—wait—that was the last office call. Let's see ... she made the last payment by mail in November, 1974, apparently from the same address. She had a follow-up visit in June, 1975, but there's no indication of another address. She apparently paid cash for that instead of being billed."

Wager carefully scratched out the "Jane Doe" on the file's lip and penned in "CROWELL, REBECCA JEAN." "Any other Crowells in the dentist's records?"

"We didn't ask. That's your job. This just came through in the evening mail."

"It's enough to move on. Thanks a lot, Fred."

The Tremont address was less than a mile from the homicide office; Wager had just pulled in to a cross town street empty of everything except blinking traffic lights when his radio called for "any homicide detective."

This shift had only one. "X-eighty-five. Go ahead."

"We have a discharged-weapon report to be filed. Corner of Quitman and Seventh."

One of the phony things about TV detectives was that they were given all the time they needed to work a single case. The television cops never juggled two or three new cases and as many old ones; they never came off the night shift with an hour to shave, shower, and shit before sitting through a long morning and even into the afternoon trying to stay awake to testify in court; they never reported two hours early to do the paperwork to meet a court deadline, or sat on their own time through the weekly closed-

72

channel telecast that covered the latest court rulings which brought changes to police procedure. And they never got turned around when they were headed for a victim's residence. "I'm on my way," Wager said.

The shooting was at the west edge of Denver near the city-county line and in an area he wasn't completely familiar with. He crossed above the street on the Sixth Avenue Freeway and saw the red flashers of the blue-and-white unit two or three blocks distant. But it took another five minutes to thread his way off the freeway and in and out of dead-end streets to the scene.

"You Detective Wager?" The officer sitting in the yellow glow of the roof-mounted flashlight peered out of the squad car at him.

"Yes. What's the story?"

The officer turned off the whipping glare of the red flashers to leave the street dark except for the living-room lights of a small house with a deep porch. "We had a ten-sixteen at this address—husband drunk and wife not drunk enough, you know the kind."

"I know." Domestic-disturbance calls were always bad news.

"Well, she phoned in the request, and when we come around that corner there, our headlights picked him up chasing her down the street with a pistol in his hand."

"You saw the weapon?"

"Son of a bitch, we did. As soon as he saw us, he opened up."

"How many shots?"

"Two or three. My partner heard three. I was on the radio and heard only two."

"Where's your partner?"

"Inside, still talking to the broad."

"The husband?"

The officer's teeth flashed. "We fired back and the fucker took off into Martinez Park. Right down there." He pointed to the dark end of the short street. "It's blacker'n shit in there—he ran smack into a tree and knocked himself silly."

"Injuries?"

"None. The fucker missed and so did we."

"How many rounds did you fire?"

"My partner fired one. I fired two." He added modestly, "He was driving—I got out of the car faster."

Wager glanced over the shooting report filled with the officer's square printing. "This looks pretty routine." The word was becoming more and more accurate to describe an officer's getting shot at; but a report like this would usually be filed at the end of the shift. "What do you want with me?"

"The wife is screaming police brutality."

"What?"

"She thinks we shouldn't have fired at hubby just because he was trying to blow our fucking heads off. She says it was our fault he ran into that tree."

"After he chased her ass down the street with a pistol?"

"Yeah. She says he does it all the time and never fired a round before tonight. She's right—we've had three or four domestic calls at this address in the last couple years. But she lays it on us that the dumb son of a bitch cold-cocked himself."

Jesus. And for that two cops stuck their necks out. Wager began taking notes on a clean page of his little green book. A policeman really had to like the job for itself; it was harder than hell to like the people involved. "All right, let's start with the names and addresses." The patrolman was right to call for an investigator as soon as possible. Weaker charges than this had been known to stick like shit on a shoe, and it didn't take more than one or two such incidents to make a man a target inside as well as outside the department. In fact, right now Wager could think of one detective who was suspected of being an animal.

7

The shooting began a busy night. Following that came a burglary in progress, a disturbance call in the Curtis Park area, a request from a patrolman for procedural help in questioning a minor, and a known-dead report that turned out to be natural causes but still required paperwork to clear it from the division's statistics. By the time Wager filed his end-of-tour reports, the Wednesday sun lay two hours high and heavy crosstown traffic choked the one-way streets that sliced up the old neighborhood surrounding the Crowell address. The apartment was in one of the last private homes on the block, the rest replaced either by rambling three-story apartments built in the 1930s for lung patients and later converted to general use, or by the newer concrete apartment towers that dwarfed the few trees left along the red stone curbs with their rusted iron rings for tying horses.

As Wager crossed the creaking boards of the front porch, he met the tang of bacon and coffee and his stomach reminded him that he had again forgotten to eat during the eight-hour tour. In a rusty row beside the front door were tacked three old-fashioned mailboxes. Two of the slips of paper wedged in the boxes' gritty slots were new; the other was yellow and brittle and bore, in faded purple ink, "Dove, G. N." The Crowell name was not posted. Wager tried the curtained front door; it opened into a paneled box that had doors on each side and a dark flight of carpeted stairs leading up to a third door. The Dove apartment was number 1.

He knocked for five minutes, shifting from one foot to another, smelling the indefinable odors that seeped from the oak panels. The old home was well built and very quiet except for occasional squeaks in the ceiling as someone above moved back and forth in a morning ritual. At last the spring lock clicked and a second bolt slid back; the door opened a crack to show two noses: one white and fleshy, at eye level; one dark and wet and growling, at knee level.

"Who is it?"

"Detective Wager, Denver Police. Are you the landlady here, ma'am?"

"I might be. What is it you want?"

"I'd like to ask some questions about a tenant of yours."

"Them Willcoxes? Is it them Willcoxes again? I told them last time I didn't have to put up with them bringing the police in here. If that's the kind of people they are, they can just move across the street. They don't care who they rent to over there!"

"It's about Rebecca Jean Crowell, ma'am."

"Crowell? Crowell? She don't live here no more."

"Can you tell me when she did live here?"

"Maybe. Why you want to know? What's she gone and done?"

"She may be the victim of a homicide, lady. I want to find out."

The eye bulged to show a pale blue iris in a yellow and bloodshot ball. "Victim? Does that mean dead?"

"Yes." Wager clenched the corners of his mouth up into what he hoped was a friendly smile. He was tired, he was hungry, he did not want to waste time getting a *duces tecum* warrant that would give him the legal right to search the landlady's records. "I want you to help us out. I want to know how long she lived here and where she might have moved."

"What you want and what you get's two different things. What's your name?"

"Wager."

"You just wait a minute, Wager. I'm calling the police to see if you're telling true."

"That's a smart thing to do, lady."

"You think I don't know that?" The door shut, the wet black nose at Wager's knee giving a snort of quick pain.

Two or three minutes later it cracked open again, the white nose poking out further than the black nose this time. "She lived here from May of 1974 to November of 1975."

"Do you know where she moved to?"

"No. They come and go. It ain't my business as long as they pay their rent and have decent ways."

"Did you forward any mail to her?"

"Not that I recollect. She didn't get much, anyway."

"Did she have many visitors?"

"Not that I know of. And that means none. I keep an eye on what goes on in my house, mister, and I don't let rooms to hussies."

"Yes, ma'am. Do you know where she worked?"

"I know she paid her rent in advance each and every month. That's all. I ain't nosy like you are, young man."

Wager forced another smile, hoping it didn't look the way it felt. "Can't you tell me anything about her?"

"Like what?"

"Where she came from. If she had next of kin in town. What she did on weekends—her hobbies—that kind of thing."

"She worked days. She said she went to some kind of school or other at night. She stayed pretty much to herself and she stayed quiet. The way I like them. Like I said, I ain't nosy. You got all you want?"

No, but that was all she was going to give him. He finished writing. "Thank you, ma'am."

The door thumped shut.

Wager pulled in to the already crowded lot of a Cowboy Bob's Chuckwagon, finally able to have breakfast—or supper—a little after nine. At ten, he used the pay telephone in a leatherette corner of the diner to call the office of Crowell's dentist. They were open; he could come over any time before five. He hung up and turned to the Crowell listings in the telephone book's white pages. No "Rebecca," no "R. J." If she had an unlisted number, it would take half a day's paperwork to run it down.

The dentist's receptionist, wearing a crisp white uniform whose tidiness flattened breast and hip, said "Good morning" as he entered a softly lit room. A large fish tank filled one wall, and small tables beside thick chairs held *National Geographic, U.S. News & World Report, Jack and Jill;* from somewhere came the kind of music that was full of violins and half-familiar melody. It was a hell of a lot richer dentist's office

79

than any he had ever gone to.

"I'm Detective Wager. I called a few minutes ago."

"You got here fast!" Her dark ponytail swung as she pressed a button on a white intercom. "I'll tell Dr. Miller you're here."

Wager looked at the pictures in half of a *National Geographic* before the dentist came out wiping his hands. He was as short as Wager and his lank gray hair was brushed straight back from his forehead. "You're from the police?"

He showed his badge. "Yes, sir."

Dr. Miller glanced at it and nodded briskly. "All right, Marie. He can see the records." He was gone again.

At the bottom of the small stack of papers inside Rebecca Crowell's folder lay an application for credit dated September, 1974. Wager began copying the personal information from the little blocks filled in by precise, erect letters in dark blue ink. It was not the kind of handwriting which indicated the applicant imagined that within two years a cop would be reading it, that the cop would be trying to find out who she was and who killed her. Hell, how many of us knew where we'd be two years from now?

The listed residence was the Tremont address, and, as Baird said, it was not updated. But she did state her place of work and her bank—Dr. Miller didn't give easy credit without hard questions: Rocky Mountain Tax & Title Service, Petroleum Building, Room 785. Job title: typist. Bank account in Central of Denver, also located downtown. Income: $425 per month, no major outstanding debts. She owned a car—a 1970

Mustang, no license listed. And, Wager knew, she had not applied for a Colorado driver's license—which was not unusual if she was new to the state. A lot of newcomers forgot about getting a new license until the old one expired. The block for parent or guardian was blank, but an emergency address listed a Mr. and Mrs. F. G. Crowell, 810 Kiowa Avenue, Kansas City, Kansas. Wager copied it and put off thinking of that for a while. Total cost of the dental work contracted for: $1,800. Payments were arranged at $500 for the first payment, $35 a month thereafter. It surprised him that no interest was charged. Little check marks showed that during the first year of treatment, she paid the stipulated amount; then she began paying $50 a month for eight months. The last payment, three months after her final checkup, was a lump sum of $580—which was pretty good on a typist's salary. "Miller doesn't charge interest on his credit deals?"

The receptionist smiled to show a thin silver wire across teeth that were, to Wager's eyes, perfectly straight. "Most orthodontists don't—it would put the price too high for many clients."

Wager thought it was too high anyway; but maybe Miller's goldfish ate a lot. "Did you ever talk with Miss Crowell about her friends or acquaintances?"

She shook her head. "I didn't work here then."

"Can I see the doc for a couple minutes?"

"I'll find out if he's finished with his patient yet." She came back in a moment. "He's casting a mold. It'll be about five minutes."

In the long silence, Wager watched the fish dart and pause among the slender grass and streams of bubbles rising from ceramic divers and sunken ships. Rebecca Crowell had paid a lot of money to have pretty teeth. On a typist's income of $425 a month: rent, transportation, clothes, taxes, night school, food—and one hell of a lot of money for pretty teeth. There had to be extra income from somewhere. How does a pretty girl make a few extra bucks?

"You wanted to see me?" Miller was wiping his hands again.

"Did Miss Crowell ever talk about herself? About her plans?"

"Lord—it's been a long time." Miller rubbed his forehead with the well-scrubbed fingers. "She never said much, but I don't remember that she was shy. More, that she just didn't talk about herself."

"Did she ever mention going to night school?"

"Not that I remember."

"How about friends? Did she mention any names?"

"None that I remember. Most patients talk about their teeth—that's why they're here. Sorry."

The Petroleum Building's small lobby opened from a busy corner of Sixteenth Street, an easy walk to the state capitol for oilmen and legislators. Wager found the Rocky Mountain Tax & Title Service on the directory and pushed the elevator button for floor seven. The company's quiet offices were marked by a frosted-glass door and large gilt letters.

"Yes, sir?" This receptionist also had her hair pulled back into a ponytail, but it was blond. And instead of an efficient uniform, she wore a soft brown sweater that, in its own way, was just as efficient.

"I'm Detective Wager, Denver Police. I'm trying to get some information on a Miss Rebecca Jean Crowell, who works here—or who used to work here."

"Rebecca? Why? What's happened?"

He'd never found an easy way to say it. "She's a homicide victim."

"Rebecca? Oh, God!" Her hands jumped to her mouth, scattering a pile of legal documents from the typing stand. "My God!"

"What's the matter?" A tall man in his mid-forties poked his head through an inner doorway. "What's wrong, Lisa?"

"This . . . this is a policeman. He says Rebecca's been killed!"

Wager showed his badge. "I understand Miss Crowell worked here?"

"She used to," said the man. "She quit about six months ago." His gray eyes stared at Wager. "You're certain it was Rebecca?"

"The dental records gave positive identification."

"Good Lord. How . . . what happened?"

"She was stabbed to death."

"Good Lord!"

The blonde, blinking back tears, scrabbled at the spilled documents; both Wager and the man quickly bent to help her.

"Did you get the one who did it?" he asked.

"Not yet. We're trying to find him. Maybe you can give me some information about her."

"Certainly! Anything."

The tall man's name was Pitkin, William N., part

owner and executive director of Rocky Mountain Title. Residence: 5958 Radcliffe Avenue, Cherry Hills Village, an area that had few hills and was nothing like a village; it was an incorporated enclave of very expensive homes on the south side of Denver. He had moved to Colorado from New York almost twenty years ago, and had known Miss Crowell only during the time she'd worked there.

The blonde was Lisa Dahl, 7011 F, Hampden West. It wasn't until she stood clutching the wad of legal sheets that Wager saw how large the woman was. Not badly proportioned, just big. She stacked the papers and then fumbled in a bottom file drawer for the employee records.

Pitkin cleared his throat and read from the folder she handed him. "Rebecca started work here in late April, 1974. Her first paycheck was for the week of April 25th."

Wager moved around to read over Pitkin's shoulder.

"She was very good. The next year she was promoted from typist to secretary."

"Can you tell me what her salary was?"

"Why, yes—ah, she began at four hundred and twenty-five dollars a month, and was raised to five twenty-five in December, 1974, then to six hundred and fifty in June, 1975, when she was promoted to administrative secretary."

Which helped explain the lump-sum settlement of the orthodontist's bill. "That's a good raise in a little over a year."

"She was a very good worker," said Pitkin. "Excellent, in fact."

"Do you know if she had any other income?"

"No, I don't."

Wager might have caught something in the voice, but he wasn't sure. "No idea at all? You're certain?"

"Of course I'm certain!"

Miss Dahl went to stand by the window and stare into the busy street below, dabbing occasionally at her eyes with a tissue.

"Did she have any particular friends? A boyfriend, maybe?"

"Not that I know of. She didn't talk much about her private life. She was a very good administrative secretary and didn't bring her home life into the office. Wouldn't you say, Lisa?"

"What? Oh, yes. She didn't speak much about herself."

Pitkin studied the blonde's face a moment. "Why don't you take the day off—I can handle things."

"You're sure? I mean—it's such a shock. . . ."

The tall man smiled gently, the flat planes of his thin cheeks folding in two deep lines beside his mouth. "Certainly."

They watched her grope her way into the hall.

"Perhaps I should see her home." Pitkin looked after the closed door.

"She probably wants to be alone," said Wager. At least he wanted her that way for a while. "Did Miss Crowell ever talk of going to night school?"

Pitkin gave it a moment. "I don't remember. I don't think so."

"Can you tell me the date she quit working here?"

"Yes . . . ah . . . she was paid through May 31, 1976. She had two weeks vacation which she took as additional salary."

"What reason did she give for quitting?"

"Only that she had another job."

"But you don't know anything about that?"

"No. As I said, she didn't talk much about herself. She always knew what she wanted and went ahead and did it without a great deal of talk. And then, I really didn't want to ask."

"Why?"

"She was a very good employee, and I always thought we treated her quite well. I thought she liked it here. She was in line for another raise in two months."

"You took it personally that she quit?"

"I suppose you could say that. It's a small office, and we're more like friends around here. Besides, she was very experienced, and I was leaving more and more of the routine administration to her. I even hired Lisa—Miss Dahl—to take over the correspondence."

"Did she leave suddenly?"

"She gave two weeks' notice. Exactly." He looked down at the page and said, as much to himself as to Wager, "But she saved her vacation time for a full year, didn't she?"

"Do you have her address at the time she quit?"

"Yes—it's here: 2418 Tremont. Apartment 3."

Again that tiny echo of doubt. "You're sure?"

"I don't know what you mean by that, but look for yourself, Detective."

Wager did. Half hidden by Pitkin's pointing finger was a telephone number penciled by a different hand: 753–4719. "Did you know that she moved from the Tremont address in 1975?"

"Really?"

"She never mentioned moving?"

"No."

Wager glanced over the words and phrases jotted in his green notebook, fragments that he would complete after he left Pitkin and had a few minutes of silence for thought. And he gave Pitkin a few seconds of silence for thought, too. "There's nothing at all you can tell me about her private life?"

"I've said that. And I'm getting tired of repeating it."

Wager smiled. "Thanks for your time."

In his car, he radioed the dispatcher for a closed frequency; the name of a deceased person wasn't broadcast on an open police band if the family had not yet been notified. The dispatcher came back on the secure channel: "Go ahead, X-eighty-five."

"I've located the next of kin of a homicide victim, Rebecca Jean Crowell." He spelled the last name. "Her parents live in Kansas City, Kansas." After reading their full name and address, he asked, "Will the Red Cross handle it?" That would be a damn sight better than a sudden telephone call from some cop out in Denver.

"If they can't, we'll get a local law agency to. You're the officer of record?"

In the Marine Corps, it had been part of a regional recruiter's job to bring the bad news to parents or spouse; now it was often a service of the local police. Wager thought that somehow there should be more difference between civilian dying and military dying. But the only real difference was that many of the civilians didn't have a fighting chance. "Yes."

"Are you on duty now?"

"For a little while. Then they can call me at home."

"Ten-four."

The next transmission was for information from the telephone company; it took less time when a request went to them from police headquarters than from an officer in the field. The police dispatcher repeated the Crowell number back to Wager. "That's an unlisted number?"

"It could be; the victim's name wasn't in the telephone book."

"O.K. We'll be back with it."

Miss Dahl's apartment was in a multi-tower complex on Hampden Avenue, one of those newer streets that still had patches of undeveloped ranchland here and there beyond the shops and restaurants strung along each asphalt curb. Wager drove wearily in and out of parking lots until he found Building 7000. A concrete path curved through low shrubs up to the lobby that served a cluster of three towers. At midmorning, it was empty of everyone except a man pushing a noisy vacuum cleaner over the red carpet. Large soft chairs and couches were scattered around, and from the fireplace came the musty odor of newly burned paper logs. Beyond a row of eight maroon leatherette doors with round ports was the recreation area—an indoor swimming pool, a pair of tennis courts sheltered by the towers, an assortment of other rooms labeled "Pike's Peak," or "Long's Peak," or "Navajo Peak." Wager found the directory for Building 7000 and pressed the button beside "L. Dahl." After two long rings, a voice answered dully from the chrome speaker, "Yes?"

"It's Detective Wager, Miss Dahl. I'm sorry to bother you at home, but I need more information."

The speaker was silent a long moment. "I really don't feel like seeing anyone."

"I understand. But I'm pretty anxious to catch the person that killed Rebecca. Maybe you can help me out."

"I see. Well. All right. Turn left off the elevator."

The speaker clicked off, followed by a buzzer in the door whose brass plate spelled "Seven Thousand, Hampden West." Wager pushed through and the buzzer stopped rattling.

He turned left when the elevator paused at the eleventh floor. A small sign on the beige wall pointed toward apartments E, F, G, and H. Lisa Dahl's door was the second. She opened it almost immediately; her blond hair hung heavily over the shoulders of the terry-cloth bathrobe, and her eyes, wiped clean of make-up, were puffy from crying.

"I shouldn't be so upset. Rebecca and I weren't really that close. We worked together for six months or so. It's really silly to be so upset." Her eyes began to fill with tears again.

"It's a natural feeling. It's the shock."

"I suppose that's it. Excuse me." She went into the

small bathroom and Wager heard the whisk of tissue pulled from its box. "Would you like some coffee? I can make some."

"I sure would." It gave her something to do, and he did need the coffee; his legs felt clumsy and tired, and his eyes stung when he rubbed them.

Leaning against the open shelves separating the small kitchen from the living room, he looked around at the porcelain knickknacks; the healthy green plants hanging, propped, and lined up on shelves near the large window; the few books—*An Illustrated Survey of Great Music; Skiing the Rockies; Woman! Who She Is!* "You got a nice place—a swimming pool and everything."

"What? Oh—thank you. It's not worth the cost. I don't use it often."

"It does look pretty expensive."

She didn't answer.

He wandered to the curtained window beyond the plants and peeked out; a narrow balcony hung over the courtyard with its green plexiglass pool and roof and open tennis courts. "How long have you been working for the title company?"

"A little less than a year. I started in January."

"Is Denver your home?"

"No, California. I moved here with my husband. My ex-husband."

Of late, everybody seemed to have an ex-something; maybe it was true that Denver had the highest divorce rate in the country. Wager got off that topic. "And you worked with Rebecca until she quit in May?"

"Yes." She handed him a cup and saucer. "Cream or sugar?"

"No, thanks." The woman's broad hands quivered slightly, but her voice was stronger. Even in the flat slippers, she stood taller than Wager, and her heavy forearms were firm. Mid-twenties, he guessed, with the healthy regular features that California blondes seemed to grow. She lit a cigarette and, staring at the curtains, held the smoke down a long time.

"Your coffee's real good," he said.

She smiled slightly. "I'm all right now."

And she seemed to be. "Do you have any idea why Rebecca quit?"

The hesitation was only slight. "She had a new job."

"Where?"

"As a model. She'd gone to a modeling school at night and finally she began to get enough work to make a living."

That explained the mannequin quality of the head, and Wager mentally kicked himself for not thinking of that. "Do you know who she worked for?"

"No—I believe it was a new agency. A woman who was just getting started. It wasn't an established name; that's how Rebecca got the job."

"Why's that?"

"Rebecca told me that Denver only has a couple of big agencies, and they've signed most of the models. This new agency needed people, and she thought it was her big chance."

"She didn't say the woman's name?"

"She did, but I really can't remember. It was so long ago."

"Did you know Rebecca's address?"

"No."

"You never went to visit her?"

"No."

"I guess she was a pretty woman—being a model and all."

Miss Dahl shrugged. "She was attractive, but not really pretty. She seemed to take a good picture."

"You saw some?"

"She showed me a set of proofs once. They were part of the modeling course."

"When was that?"

"A little while after I started working. Perhaps six or eight weeks."

"So she planned for a long time to be a model?"

"She said that was the only thing she really wanted. She was that way—when she wanted something, she worked very hard for it."

"Those modeling schools are pretty expensive, aren't they?"

"I don't know. I suppose they charge what they can get."

"Did she have any other income that you know of?"

"No. Maybe from her parents. Maybe she had money from them."

Wager took the last sip of coffee from the cup whose handle was too small for his fingers. "Mr. Pitkin seemed surprised that she quit so suddenly."

"I don't know about that."

"But you weren't surprised by it?"

"Not really. Rebecca was that way, too."

"What way?"

"When she didn't want something any more, she dropped it. A lot of people are that way."

"Did she ever tell you anything about her personal life? Did she have many friends?"

"I don't think so. She knew some people, I suppose; she went to some parties and sometimes went skiing. We talked about skiing, and I think she belonged to a ski club. But she didn't say much about herself. She was very independent—sometimes I almost envied her. I think she preferred to listen to me instead."

"Why's that?"

"My divorce. It was just starting when I began work. I . . . I needed someone to talk to. Most of my friends are in California. Rebecca was a good listener—she sympathized but not enough to . . . lose perspective. It's strange how sometimes it's easier to talk to someone like that rather than to a good friend."

"Did Rebecca have any boyfriends?"

"None that I know of."

"You're sure?"

"Yes."

He stared down at the little swirl of dried coffee on the bottom of his cup. "Not even William Pitkin?"

This time her eyes told him what she denied: "No!"

"Miss Dahl," said Wager softly, "I'm too goddamned tired to waste any more time. Rebecca was stabbed with a butcher knife and whoever did it liked his work. Pitkin didn't tell me all he knew about her, and I want you to tell me the truth."

A sudden quivering intake of breath; Wager hoped she wasn't going to cry—he was weary enough now so

that everything was an effort, especially a crying woman. But it wasn't tears that had shaken her. "Not
Bill—he wouldn't. . . . You don't think that Bill—?"

"No," lied Wager. "But I do want to know everything about the victim. I want to know so I can find
who did kill her."

She suddenly stood and walked the three or four
steps across the living room, her fingers tangled together in front of her heavy chest. Now the tears had
really started, the deep kind that came silently, and
Wager knew they weren't just for Rebecca.

"She and Bill were . . . lovers. When I first started
working there."

"Pitkin was married?"

"Yes." She looked down at her twisted fingers. "He
still is."

Wager tried to keep his voice neutral, to mask the
pull of a weariness that went far beyond fatigue. "Tell
me about it."

Her voice grew thin and sounded as flat as Wager
felt. "I'm not certain. They broke up a few months
before she left. She didn't say why and I didn't ask."

"Did Pitkin give her money?"

"Yes." She said bitterly, "That seems to be his usual
arrangement."

"Are you and him lovers, Miss Dahl?"

"Yes."

"Was that before or after Rebecca left?"

The sloping shoulders of the bathrobe bobbed
once. "Before. But they weren't seeing each other any
more. Bill and I had lunch a few times, a drink or
two; it just happened." Sudden anger narrowed her

eyes. "It doesn't make any difference to anyone except us! We're two people who need each other that way, and that's all it will ever be! I'm not asking for anything more—I've tried being married and it was a hell of a lot worse than this!"

"Did Rebecca leave because of you and Pitkin?"

"No! She left because she wanted to be a model. That's all she ever wanted. And I wish *you* would leave!"

"Was Pitkin at work all day on October 19th?"

She stared at Wager and her face drained to a pale yellow. "You said you didn't suspect him."

"It has to be asked."

"That was a Tuesday—we were both there."

"Did you go out to lunch with him?"

She thought back. "No. He had a business lunch that day. But he was back before a two-o'clock appointment."

"Do you know if he went home that night?"

"I know he did not."

"He didn't?"

"He was with me."

"At night? Late?"

"All night. Here."

Wager could no longer tell if she lied.

8

The dispatcher's call reached him in the apartment tower's parking lot; the unlisted number from Crowell's employment record was located at 5400 East Jewell, Building G, Apartment 16. Wager thought it was a complex less than half a mile away, and when he reached the address, he was right; it was one of a series of red brick buildings lining the Valley Freeway, all three stories high and sitting like military barracks—the kind that's always seen but never noticed. He wound past aging but tenacious little homes filling in around newer commercial sites that had sprung up on the residential streets pinched off between Colorado Boulevard and the Valley Freeway. Finally, he located the alley leading to Building G. It seemed that expensive apartments had a street number for each unit, while cheaper ones had a single number for the whole complex. All the units in this complex were 5400 East Jewell.

Among the line of mailboxes recessed into the wall beside the entry was one labeled in familiar erect letters, "Crowell, R. J." The glimmer of three or four envelopes showed through slots in the scratched brass lid. Just inside the entry, a sign pointed down to the "Garden Level" apartments, numbers 1–19. The tunnel-like hallway was carpeted and dimly lit by widely spaced wall lamps; a square of frosted light and a red exit sign gleamed at the far end. The lifeless air smelled of a curious mixture of new glue and old dust; from some vague direction among the thin walls came the rhythmic thump of a stereo's loud bass, and beneath that the blurred rattle of daytime television. No one answered his knock; even the silence felt stale. He went back to the car to radio a request to the police lab.

"This is X-eighty-five—I've got an apartment I'd like you to look at." He told them the address.

"Is it an emergency?"

"No. But it's the residence of a homicide victim. I'd like fingerprints, vacuum samples—the complete survey."

"It'll probably take a couple hours before we can get there."

That meant they wouldn't complete a sweep of the apartment until five or so. "Ten-four." He went in search of the complex's manager.

"Yes? Want to look at a unit?" Wager was surprised that the man was only in his twenties. A thin six two, he wore gold-rimmed glasses and had the start of a sand-colored goatee over the bony point of his chin.

"Number G-16." G-16, E-20, X-85—Wager began to feel as if he were calling a goddamned bingo game. He flashed his badge. "Can you tell me the name of that apartment's renter?"

The young man glanced at the badge and looked up the information without any crap about subpoenas or rights to privacy. "Rebecca J. Crowell. She got a discount because she signed a year's lease. In fact, it was up on Monday, October 25th, the day before yesterday."

"Her rent was paid on time?" He knew what the answer would be.

"Yep."

"She's been identified as a homicide victim. I'd like to see the apartment."

The fuzzy jaw sagged. "Homicide? Here?"

It took place somewhere. "I'd like to see."

"My gosh! Just a minute." He flipped a recording switch on his telephone and grabbed a heavy ring of keys from the peg above a desk. "You don't need any kind of papers for this, do you?"

Wager didn't think so; anyway, the renter wouldn't complain. "No."

The manager led him down a short cut of narrow back walks past trash dumpers overflowing behind board screens. "It's just over here. Man, it's hard to believe something like that happening around here!"

"Why?"

"We got nice folks here. Young couples, people just getting started." The narrow head shook from side to side. "It's really hard to believe."

"Did you know Miss Crowell?"

"I had to fix her plumbing once." Wager looked at him and the man's face turned bright red beneath its fuzz. "Not like that, man! I mean her apartment. We got *nice* people living here, or I wouldn't work here."

Wager waited until the manager unlocked the door. "Don't come in—I want it undisturbed for the lab people. Don't open this door for anybody but more cops."

"Sure." The gold-rimmed glasses peeked this way and that, trying to see past Wager. "Anything else you want, I'm in the next building over."

"Thanks."

Wager was very tired now, at that state when the mind wearily slides off the point it tries to focus on and wanders among loosely related thoughts. He closed the door and just stood looking around the boxy apartment. It was like so many others in so many other complexes: nude cubicles designed for quick turnover and easy painting, little squares that swallowed up any attempt to make them personal. Rebecca had tried plants and pictures, but they only looked temporary. The walls were almost covered with prints, some of which Wager even recognized: a Spanish city on an elongated hill and lit by yellow and brown light; a blue-green pond filled with lily pads that looked fuzzy; a dark painting of unconnected lines that seemed to be a man changing into a guitar or vice versa. On the wide ledge at the windows that started two-thirds of the way up the wall sat a long row of large plants: lacy fern shoots dangling down, split-leaf philodendrons springing out on thick stems, fat purple-leaved plants that Wager remembered from his mother's living room, elongated leaves pointing up in a spray of sharp tips. Wager had that strange feeling of seeing all this for the second time, and then he realized it was the plants—they reminded him of Lisa Dahl's apartment. And of the Botanic Gardens.

Wandering without touching anything, he worked his way to the bathroom to gently flip the light switch. It was clean, and only when he saw that did he realize he had been holding his breath.

He peered at the sink, the tiles, the tub. The lab people would have to make certain, of course, but Wager scraped the blade of his pocketknife in the crack around the bathtub drain. There were none of the crusty black flakes of old blood. No stains anywhere else; no pale, freshly cleaned spots on rug or tiles. The butchering had not taken place here. Careful not to move anything until the lab people had their chance, he looked through the closets and dressing table in the space between bath and bedroom. Shoes—some thirty pairs, it looked like—stood toe against the wall beneath a closet bar crowded with dresses arranged by color. A woman would know better than he what that meant, but Wager vaguely remembered the way his ex-wife hung her clothes—the most used near the open end, the least used gradually slipping down the bar into forgotten space. In this closet, with its careful arrangement of dresses and shoes, there seemed to be no forgotten space.

After wrapping a handerchief around his fingers, he opened the small refrigerator; a half-gallon of skim milk that smelled sour, wilted vegetables, a few packages of lean meat, eggs; cans of orange juice in the freezer. In none of the cabinets did he find alcohol; her last drink—like her last everything—took place somewhere else. At last, in the wire tray under the telephone stand, he found what all this neatness and order had told his subconscious to look for: an appointment book.

The few names in it were first names, men and women; but the page for October 19th was blank. He thumbed through the other dates; at the back was a short list of names and telephone numbers. One of them was Bill—he cross-checked "Pitkin" and "Rocky Mountain Tax & Title" in the telephone book. The number was for Pitkin's home telephone, and his name appeared twice in her calendar—early in June and in mid-August. Wager wondered if the other men's names were the same relationship. Some entries were more cryptic: "A.I., 7:30"; "E's, 6–8." Beginning in mid-February, the cryptic entries became more frequent, going up into mid-November—appointments that she would not be keeping now. One set of initials, "A.I.," appeared every Thursday at the same time through December 22nd. Someone, somewhere, had not met her last Thursday, would not meet her again (tomorrow); and five other appointments had been missed since she was killed. Yet no one had filed a missing-persons report. Whoever she had appointments with—men?—couldn't complain when she didn't show up.

He left a note in the wire tray for the lab people's record: "One appointment book, Wager." Slipping it into his pocket, he opened the drawers of her precisely arranged bureau. In the top right one he found a loose-leaf notebook filled with clear plastic envelopes. The first twenty or so contained pictures of Rebecca Crowell and, despite Lisa Dahl's statement, Wager thought she was very pretty indeed. The remaining envelopes were empty.

Some of the plastic sheets of photographs were a series of twenty or so small pictures. All were black-and-white and taken against an empty background that had the shadowless clarity of studio work. On other pages, color and black-and-white enlargements of particular poses ranged from evening gowns to bathing suits. Some were awkward and tense—even Wager could see that in the strained smile or the unnatural twist of body or fingers. But most were graceful, all showed a very pretty girl apparently enjoying the camera; none of them looked like the thing that had been found in the Botanic Gardens.

Maybe it was that thought, maybe it was the hour; whichever, the weariness suddenly fell on him like a heavy blanket, and he wanted to get out of the hot, close air of the stale apartment. Choosing one of the full-face poses in a black evening dress, he slipped another note for the lab people into the plastic envelope: "I took this one for I.D. use, Wager." On the back of the stiff photograph, a stamped credit read, "High Country Profiles, 1608 North Sheridan." Each of the other photographs bore the same credit.

He set the spring lock on the apartment door as he left, and paused at the mailbox. Using the tiny wire tool he brought with him from the narc squad, Wager gently twisted open the mailbox catch. Doyle would not like to know about that tool, but—and Wager smiled to himself—this was out of the bulldog's jurisdiction: it was a federal crime. Three envelopes: one addressed to occupant, one a bill from Neusteter's, the third an oil company bill—which brought into focus something at the edge of his mind: the parking slot for Apartment 16 was vacant. He radioed the Traffic Division requesting any up-to-date numbers for the Ford registered in the Crowell name. He thought the reply would take longer, but it came before he was halfway back to his apartment.

"We list the vehicle as a 1970 Ford Mustang. The '76 Colorado license is AR-3753. No warrants."

"Can you put that on a ten-ninety-nine?" He shouldn't say it was stolen, but that was one way to find out where it was.

"Ten-four."

9
———

The telephone dredged him out of one of those heavy sleeps that gum the eyes shut and push the mind somewhere deep into a muffled rush of sound. His room held the remaining gray of early dusk, and the illuminated clock by his bed said 4:45. He knocked the receiver to the rug, groped, and finally pulled it to him by the cord.

"Wager."

"Is this Detective Wager of the Denver Police Department?"

He wondered dimly why telephone operators always had that clipped, nasal voice. "Yes."

"Go ahead, please."

A second voice came on, male, elderly, hesitant. "Is this Detective Wager?"

"Yes, yes, it is."

"I'm calling about my daughter Rebecca Crowell. They said you maybe could tell me something about what happened to her?"

It took Wager a deep breath or two. "I can't tell you much, Mr. Crowell, because I don't know much yet. They did tell you she was a homicide victim?"

"They told me. I thought maybe you could tell me how . . . why . . ."

"She was stabbed, sir. We don't know yet who did it." The remnants of sleep were gone now. "Did she ever write you about any friends or acquaintances she had here?"

"Not that I recollect." A hand covered the mouthpiece and Wager could imagine him repeating the question to his wife. Their living room would be dark—perhaps a small light by the telephone—and the wife would have a handerchief wadded in her hand. "No. She wrote regular—once a week, just as regular. But she only asked about folks here... school friends and such...." The voice trembled and pulled away.

"Mr. Crowell? Can I ask you another question, Mr. Crowell?"

"Yes. Go ahead—I'm here."

"Did you send her money?"

"Money? No. Rebecca was independent. She wouldn't be beholden. She kept saying she was doing fine. We thought she was doing fine."

"Yes, sir. I'll find out what mortuary she's been sent to and ask them to contact you about arrangements and such." And the undertaker could tell the parents about the closed coffin, too. "I'm sorry about her death, sir."

"I just don't understand.... Her mother and me, we just... It just seems..."

Wager finished the sentence in his mind: unfair. "Yes, sir. As soon as I find out anything, we'll let you know." He didn't want to sound so official, but it came out that way. Words were never enough. Nor gestures. Nothing was ever enough. And anyway, when you got to the bottom of it all, the only reality was silence.

Still in bed, he called the morgue for the name of

the mortuary, then dialed that number and gave Mr. Crowell's address to the hushed voice that said, "Thank you, Officer."

He made a pot of coffee, perking it once and boiling it for the hard taste he liked. With a steaming cup under his nose, he telephoned the Rocky Mountain Title office before they closed. "Mr. Pitkin? This is Detective Wager. I want to talk to you again."

The line hummed for a long moment. "Lisa called me."

"Then you know what it's about."

"Excuse me." The voice said "Be right with you" to someone. "I may know. But I may not want to."

Wager swallowed a mouthful of burning coffee. "You don't have to if you don't want—that's true. But, Pitkin, I can fix it so you have to talk in open court."

"Are you threatening me?"

"Yes. With the law."

"Listen, can I call you back? It's hellish around here without a secretary."

"Does your office close at five?"

"It sure will today."

"Then you meet me at the Frontier around five-thirty. You know where it's at?"

Pitkin was surprised. "Sure. Down on Curtis Street."

"I'll be in the back room. Five-thirty."

The rambling, many-roomed tavern was, of course, crowded at this time of the afternoon. As Wager picked his way through the elbows and chairs jamming the main lounge, Red, the bartender, jerked his head with a hurried "How's by you, Gabe," and filled the counter's service space with a forest of beer mugs. Wager saw familar faces either in uniform or plainclothes scattered through the dim room; and he also caught sliding glimpses of a few other faces that were occasionally seen in station houses. The crowd had spilled into the back room, but he cornered a seat at his favorite booth near the noisy kitchen window. Rosie trotted past with a tray of empty dishes and gave him a quick smile. "Be with you in a minute, Gabe."

He had started a second beer before Pitkin stood frowning in the dim light of the doorway. Wager wagged an arm and the man came over, a tall figure moving with nervous quickness. "Sit down. I'm glad you made it. It saves trouble for both of us."

Pitkin glanced at the crowded tables. "This is a strange place to be—ah—interrogated."

"Who's interrogating anybody? I'm just asking for a little help with a homicide victim."

"I'm here because I have no choice."

"Yeah. That's true." Wager gestured to Rosie. "I'm having something to eat. How about you?"

"I eat later. At home."

But he did have a martini—very dry, made with Bombay gin. Wager waited until Pitkin had a long sip. "So Rebecca Crowell was your mistress."

"Friend. The word's 'friend' now."

Wager cut into the floured tortilla wrapping of a large burrito. "All right—'friend.' And your new friend is Miss Dahl."

A slight twist of Pitkin's thin lips. "She was until this

afternoon. I'm not sure how we feel about it now."

"You're married?"

"Of course. And very happily. Does that surprise you?"

Some things still surprised Wager, but not that. "Did your wife find out about Miss Crowell?"

"No. And I hope she doesn't. It would hurt her." He gazed levelly at Wager.

"I'm interested in homicide, not adultery. And you'd better give me the truth from now on."

"I thought this wasn't an interrogation?"

Wager smiled. "You're not under oath, you haven't been warned of your rights. What you tell me can't be brought into court." Maybe. He folded the little green notebook flat at a page and peered at it. "You said this afternoon you didn't know she moved from the Tremont address."

"I—ah—lied."

"I know that. What I don't know is how many other things you lied about." He gestured for refills. "Let's you start all over again."

Pitkin rolled the martini's olive around in his mouth before chewing it. Then he shrugged. "It's nothing unusual. A couple of months after she started working for me, we went to bed. It was nice, so we did it some more."

"A lot?"

"Once or twice a month. That was as much as we wanted." Again that little twist of the lips. "It wasn't a greatly passionate affair—I guess you could call it functional. We were functional friends."

"Did she want you to divorce your wife and marry

her?"

"Oh, no. She never mentioned that. Rebecca had her own plans, and marriage wasn't in them."

"Plans like what?"

"She thought she could be a model."

"Couldn't she?"

"I . . . No, I don't really think she could. Not a good one. She was photogenic; you've probably seen some of her proofs. But the kind of"—he groped for the word with one of the few gestures Wager had seen him use—"life, or warmth, or sensuality—whatever it is—that a top model projects, she just didn't have it."

"Do you know a lot about models?"

"I've known a few."

"Friends?" Wager tried not to sound impressed, but Pitkin heard it.

"Of course." He smiled.

"At the same time that Crowell was your friend?"

"No."

Wager wondered if Pitkin was just interested in having an extra woman around, rather than liking any quality of a particular woman. "Did Rebecca Crowell have any other 'friends' while she was with you?"

"Not that I know of. Though I could scarcely object if she did. Besides, neither of us was jealous of the other. It really wasn't that kind of relationship."

Wager suspected that argument was more often one of empty words than of real feeling. But coming from this man, it might be true; whatever Pitkin felt didn't seem strong enough to cause jealousy. "You knew she left the Tremont address."

"I wanted her to. But not for that dump she moved into. That was, I guess the only thing we ever argued about."

"Let's hear it."

"Well, the first few times, we went to motels. But that's . . . sordid. I wanted her to have her own apartment—with privacy. A nice place; I was willing to pay for it."

"The Tremont place wasn't private?"

"I never went there. Rebecca said the landlady was a real bitch."

Wager went along with that. "Why didn't you like the new one?"

"It was a dump. I gave her enough money for a nice apartment—I was thinking of something like Hampden West. Instead, she leased that Jewell Avenue place."

Hampden West was Lisa Dahl's address. Both she and Crowell had moved near the corner of town where Pitkin lived; apparently, the man didn't like long commutes. "Do you remember the rents?"

"I gave her three hundred and twenty-five dollars a month; the place she rented was a hundred and forty."

"Did you keep paying the three twenty-five after she took the cheaper place?"

"Certainly. I told her I'd pay that much rent if she moved out of the Tremont apartment." The mouth twitched as he gazed past Wager's shoulder at some memory. "After I saw the dump she rented, I was really teed off. As I said, it was the only time we had an argument. And then it wasn't much."

"How's that?"

"All she said was 'You told me you'd pay three hundred and twenty-five if I moved out; I never said I'd spend that much.' She was right—and a deal's a deal."

Lisa Dahl probably had to sign a contract that said where she would live. "What did Crowell do with the extra money?"

"She paid her orthodontist bills and took some more modeling lessons. And she bought clothes. She thought of clothes as an investment."

Given her raises, given an extra $185 a month, she might have squeezed all those payments out. Maybe. "Did she have any other income at all?"

"I gave her money now and then—as a gift. Christmas, birthdays... anniversaries—she wanted money instead of things."

"How much?"

"Three or four hundred. A couple of times a year. Sometimes she got stuck at the end of the month and I'd help out. But don't get the idea she was greedy—if I didn't have it, I told her; if I did, I gave it. Hell, what's money for?"

Wager leaned back in the booth and sipped at the beer. "Did she ever threaten to tell your wife?"

"Rebecca? No! She wasn't a blackmailer, Detective Wager. In fact, sometimes when I wanted to give her money, she wouldn't take it; if she didn't need it, she wouldn't take it. When she had enough, she'd pick up the check for dinner—it made her feel good." Pitkin smiled again. "Equal."

"You said it bothered you when she left."

"It did. And I'm still a little upset. I suppose I shouldn't be, though."

"You had a businesslike arrangement. What bothered you?"

"I suppose that's what upset me—it turned out to be too businesslike. We were always open with each other. I like that in my women. And she made no demands on my time or affections, had none of those dreams about marrying me someday. But it really was a shock to get a typed two-week notice on letterhead stationery! It was as if all along she had a goal that, when she reached it, would 'terminate our contract.' Maybe I got some of my own medicine, you think?"

"Did Lisa Dahl know of your arrangement with Crowell?"

"If she didn't then, she did later. She asked me about it."

"But that wasn't until after Crowell quit the job?"

"Lisa and I became friends just before Rebecca left—when she and I weren't seeing each other any more. I think Lisa told you that already."

"And now you've got the same kind of business deal with Miss Dahl?"

Pitkin did not hesitate. "Yes. But Lisa is far more emotional. I'm afraid she still has romantic illusions." He drained his glass. "Maybe it was too soon after her divorce. I think women don't realize just how alone they really are after a divorce."

Pitkin knew a hell of a lot more about the subject than Wager did; he probed once more in a different direction. "Did you ever see Crowell again after she quit?"

112

This time there was hesitation; Wager studied his suddenly restless eyes.

Finally, "Yes."

"For sex?"

Pitkin wagged his head. "In a way."

"What the hell does that mean?"

"We had sex, yes. But it was as much for old times' sake as anything else. We had dinner and then went back to that damned apartment for a drink and a good-to-see-you-how-are-you talk. The sex was as much a part of the talk as . . . as the drinks were."

"How many times did you see her?"

"Twice. Once a little while after she quit, once a few months ago."

"Did she call you?"

"No, she wouldn't do that. I called her. I guess I wanted to know if it had really been that businesslike."

"Had it?"

"In a nice way. But yes, it sure was." Pitkin may have laughed.

"How long ago did you last see her?"

"I can't recall for certain. Three months? Last June or July? I really can't tell you."

In the girl's appointment book, the dates had been in June and August. Wager was very careful with the next question. "Did Lisa Dahl know?"

"No."

"You're that certain?"

"Yes. She would have said something. She's the kind of woman who couldn't keep quiet about something like that. And, as I said, I encourage openness."

"Is it possible that Crowell told her?"

Again Pitkin shook his head. "Lisa would have said something. While she's not jealous of my wife, I'm certain she'd be very bitter if I had another friend. As I told you, she's very emotional."

Wager ordered a last round and waited while Rosie cleared his dishes and quickly told him that her oldest daughter was just starting college. She was going to be a teacher, Rosie said proudly.

"When you saw Crowell those two times, did she ask you for money?"

"No. In fact, one time she bought the dinner. She'd made some money modeling."

"Did you go to a restaurant? Do you remember its name?"

"The Chanticleer. I—ah—go there a lot with friends."

"Have you ever been to the Botanic Gardens?"

"Where? Botanic Gardens?" The puzzlement seemed genuine.

Wager nodded.

"No. That's one of those places you think about visiting but never get around to."

"You don't like plants much?"

The puzzled look slowly cleared. "Ah—Rebecca's jungle! She really did like plants—had pet names for them, kept them snipped and washed or whatever plant lovers do. The only thing I could figure out was that they were there when she wanted them, and when she didn't, they didn't bother her. Rebecca would like that about them."

"You didn't argue over them?"

114

"Plants? How in God's name can anyone argue over plants? It was her apartment to fix up any way she wanted to."

Wager had seen no plants at Rocky Mountain Title—not even near the secretary's desk where, in most offices, they would be found. But Lisa Dahl's apartment had a few.

"Does Miss Dahl like plants, too?"

"Not like Rebecca. Or she can't grow them as well."

"How about telling me where you were on October 19th."

"Lisa told me you asked her that, too. You have her quite worried. The answer's the same—I was at work all day, and then with her. All night. I arranged an overnight business trip."

"You're certain that was the night of October 19th?"

"Positive. That's our anniversary—Lisa's and mine. We celebrated."

Wager wondered how Pitkin could keep all the anniversaries separate.

Like all cops, Wager had grown a good nose for smelling lies; and though Pitkin wanted to lie every now and then, Wager could swear he had told the truth. It was as if Pitkin wanted to show complete honesty about his "friends" because he wanted Wager to believe him guiltless in the Crowell murder. But his only alibi was Miss Dahl, and two people could have done the murder; or, given Lisa Dahl's size, either one of the two. Because he was her only alibi, too. But why murder the girl? Rebecca Crowell wasn't Pitkin's first mistress or his last; nor did the man show the kind of jealousy that led to murder. And if he was being blackmailed by one woman, would he turn so soon to another who might do the same thing? It just didn't fit. Unless Pitkin had something else to gain . . . perhaps by covering for Lisa Dahl. . . . Maybe the fear that if Miss Dahl was arrested, the whole tangle of Pitkin's affairs would be pulled into the newspapers.

Wager drove into a gas station that had the glass box of a telephone booth on one corner, and dialed a number from his notebook. A sleepy voice answered.

"Miss Dahl? This is Detective Wager."

"I don't feel like talking."

"A couple questions." He didn't give her time to say no. "Do you know if Pitkin ever met Rebecca Crowell after she stopped working for him?" He waited. "Miss Dahl?"

"I . . . don't think he did. Maybe he did."

"But you don't know for sure?"

"I thought once I smelled her perfume on him. But I didn't ask."

"You recognized the perfume she used?"

"We worked in the same office for five months."

Wager could recognize some of his fellow officers' scents, lotions, and lack thereof. "How long ago was this?"

Her voice had a shrug in it. "A few months. I really don't remember."

"Why didn't you want to ask him about her?"

"What difference would it have made?"

"I mean, didn't you care that he might have seen her?"

"Yes. But I knew it made no difference. He meets his end of the bargain, and I meet mine. Anything else is irrelevant."

"And you're content with that?"

"You are goddamned right I am, Detective Wager." The line clicked dead.

10

He wanted to use his own telephone to chase down the numbers in Rebecca Crowell's appointment book. For one thing, the homicide office was too small to hold more than one shift, and, for another, he had no desire to listen to Ross. But before he could get started, his telephone rang.

"Gabe, the morgue people tell me they got an I.D. on that decap victim."

"That's right, Gargan. It came in earlier this morning."

"All right! What have you got for me?"

"I still don't know that much about her. Her name's Rebecca Jean Crowell." He spelled the last name. "She's unmarried, came from Kansas City, Kansas; she lived in Denver for a couple of years, and seems to have been a self-employed model."

Gargan's voice grew to the size of headlines: "Oh, yeah? A model? Any pictures?"

"They're all being held for evidence."

"Aw, shit on that noise, Wager!"

"They're evidence, Gargan. They're locked up."

"Yeah. Old buddy. Is she a registered model? Does she have an agent?"

"I'm trying to find out."

"I'll see what I can do. And if I find anything, Wager, I'll be real sure to let you know."

In the circle of the buzzing receiver, Wager could

see Gargan the Gumshoe, hat on the back of his head, cigarette smoke in one eye, nimbly outwitting the police in the relentless pursuit of truth and the public's right to know. Propping open Crowell's book, Wager dialed the listing office of the telephone company to find addresses for the numbers on the dated pages. A recording told him that it was very sorry but the office was closed after five and would be open at 8 A.M. every working day. He muttered *"Caca"* and called the police laboratory for their report on the Crowell apartment.

"The team got back just before quitting time, Detective Wager. They got some prints and hair samples and some stuff in the vacuum bags that we haven't run through testing yet. That's all."

"They didn't find her purse?"

"No. They did bring in some papers from the coffee-table drawer, but nobody's gone through them yet. If you want a look, they'll be here. As for everything else, we're working on it now and we should be finished by the time we go off duty."

"Is Baird still on the graveyard shift?"

"Right."

"Then leave the report with him. I'll see him later."

"Right."

Next, he looked up High Country Profiles in the white pages and checked it with the list in the back of Crowell's appointment book. It was there, and Wager dialed it. He was surprised to hear a man answer after a single ring: "High Country."

"This is Detective Gabriel Wager, Denver Police. Who am I talking to, please?"

Wager could have counted to ten before the voice came back, slower, slightly higher in pitch. "Who?"

"Detective Wager. Denver Police Department. Can I have your name, please?"

"Bennett. Phil Bennett. This is High Country Profiles, man. What number you calling?"

Wager told him. "Do you know a Rebecca Jean Crowell, Mr. Bennett?"

"Crowell? It doesn't pull my chain. But let me eyeball the list. Give me your number and I'll buzz you back."

"I can wait."

"Maybe you can, baby, but I can't. I'm in the dark-room, processing. Give me your number, man, and I'll call back."

"Will you be there for the next half-hour? I'll come over."

". . . All right. My place is around on the side of the building. Ring the night bell—the receptionist cut out for the day."

After he hung up, Wager read back through the men's names in the appointment book. A "Phil" appeared almost a dozen times, beginning in April and then with increasing frequency. But not on October 19th.

Through the hazy twilight of autumn, Wager saw a dim sign for High Country Profiles over a brick building that squatted by itself just off busy North Sheridan Avenue. The structure held two offices: the dark one in front repaired electronic instruments; the back—reached by an ill-lit walk leading down the

120

building's north wall—was the photography studio. The night bell had a small sign: "Ring After 5 P.M." Wager pressed it.

A click and a buzz; a voice from somewhere over a wire said, "Come in and sit down—be right there."

Wager ignored the fake-leather chair and looked around the small reception room lit by a single fluorescent ceiling light. The empty desk took up most of the space, but on the walls were large samples: a model's face framed in a scarlet shawl and staring back open-mouthed; a back-lighted female figure, nude, whose slender legs thrust into the light like a hosiery advertisement; a woman's giant profile, hair spread across a pillow. She had her mouth open, too. Between the pictures were a few awards for excellence in something or other that Wager had just started to read when he heard a curtain slide along a metal rod. A man bustled out of the hallway from the rear, rubbing a paper towel in his palms.

"You're the cop?" Bennett was a few inches taller than Wager, just under six feet; he wore an open shirt beneath a black lab apron and seemed to be in his mid-thirties. A closely trimmed black beard showed no gray, and his straight glossy hair lay sculpted around his ears and neck and had that solid look produced by hair spray. The narrow beard and cap of hair made Wager think of the Sheriff of Nottingham. "You should have laid your number on me, man— you blew a trip. I don't have any Crowells for customers." He picked up a loose-leaf account book from the receptionist's desk; a divider said "Ca–Cz." "Look for yourself, man."

Wager held out the photograph, face down. "Isn't this your stamp?"

"Hey, far out!" Bennett turned it over. "But, man, that's Tommie Lee!"

"Who?"

"Tommie Lee—a model. I do her photos and tapes." He turned the pages of the ledger. "Here." A sheet titled "Lee, Tommie" held a short series of entries followed by a credit and debit column. He looked up at Wager, pale eyes wide. "You're here for a reason, man. Lay it on me."

"Miss Crowell—Lee—has been killed."

"Oh, Jesus Christ." Bennett stared at Wager, then down at the picture of the smiling girl. "That's heavy. How'd it happen?"

"She was stabbed."

Bennett gazed at the face. "Poor Tommie. Who did it, man?"

"I'm trying to find out. I want to ask you a few questions about her."

"Sure. Anything. When did all this go down?"

"A week ago yesterday."

"That long ago? I didn't read about ... But you called her something else, didn't you?" He groped for a package of cigarettes and offered one to Wager. "I never knew her real name."

Wager didn't smoke. "How well did you know her?"

"She was a customer. I knew her like I know most of the customers."

"But only as Tommie Lee?"

A deep breath through the cigarette. "A lot of the girls use professional labels. Especially if their real

122

name doesn't grab you. And maybe there's something psychological about it. Like, they can pose better if it's not their everyday self. You know what I mean?"

"How long was she a customer?"

He jabbed out the cigarette and pointed to the top entry on her account. "April 16th was her first session." A faint ding came from the back of the shop. "My negatives are cooked. Come on—we can rap while I work."

Wager followed him into an alcove blocked off by a heavy curtain; Bennett pulled it to, and in the sudden blackness Wager heard a doorknob click. A hand guided his arm. "Just in here—the inner sanctum. Give your eyes a couple minutes, man." The door shut and gradually Wager's eyes felt rather than saw the red glow of the darkroom light. The photographer, oddly pale in the redness, carefully pulled wet strips of celluloid from a tray. The nervousness was gone, and through the dimness Bennett moved quickly and surely.

"Do you own this place, Mr. Bennett?"

"Me and my brother. But he's just an investor. He doesn't work here."

"What all do you do?"

"Everything, man. Still and motion shots, art and layout, audio work, even the copy if some dude doesn't have his own." He finished hanging the last strip of 35-millimeter film and turned to Wager, his face blank in the red glow. "I offer a full range of advertising technology, but photography's the main line. The audio end of the business is starting to move, though; I'm getting a lot of radio spot work."

"Was Miss Crowell one of your models?"

"'Miss Crowell!' That really sounds weird. No—I don't exactly have my own models. That bag is for agents. If I get an assignment where a body's needed right then, I might call one of the girls. Or a voice—a lot of times customers need a special voice, so I'll get somebody I've heard. Most of the time, the customers provide their own people through agencies."

"And that's how you met Miss Crowell?"

"No. She came in for some portfolio work. That's a major line—I'm the best in town for portfolio work."

"What's that?"

"Jesus, where've you been, man? Every model needs a portfolio for her agent to show. You know, a lot of different poses, profile shots, face-ons, the whole bit. The agent's got to show his customer that his model can demonstrate a product."

"It sounds like a lot of work—a lot of time."

"You better believe it! And a portfolio has to be updated every couple years. Even if a girl's working a lot, her agent can use only a few finished shots for the portfolio. They need a variety of poses—not everybody wants the same thing."

"Did Miss Crowell have many jobs?"

"She was starting to get a few." The pink blur of face moved from side to side. "With good training, she could have made it all the way, man."

"I thought she already had lessons."

"Shit. Those sons of bitches didn't teach her a thing about posing. I must of thrown away nine out of ten pictures at our first session. In fact, I remember I asked her if she was really serious about this modeling

124

trip—I couldn't figure anybody that bad would be that serious about it, you know?"

"What happened when you said that?"

"She didn't like to hear it. Most of these broads think they're Margaux Hemingway or somebody, and no modeling school wants to tell them different. But Tommie didn't get pissed—she just said, 'You tell me what you want and I'll do it.' And, by God, she did!"

"So she got better?"

"It took a hell of a lot of work. And a hell of a lot of money."

"Why so much?"

"Figure it out: the cost of materials plus studio time. I run a business, man, not a charity."

"Did she pay cash for it?"

"Sure. The most I give on margin is ninety days, but she always paid when due. That's why I put in a little extra. That, and she was getting good. She was really starting to groove it. God, it's too bad."

"She had an appointment with you last Friday and didn't show up. Did you try to call her?"

"If a broad misses, I don't call them; they call me. Like, I'm too busy, you know? It's their loss, not mine." The cap of hair bobbed once.

"Did she miss any other times?"

Bennett thought back, drawing his hand down the band of whiskers. "Not one time, man. A lot of the girls get last-minute jobs—that's the business—so they might miss a session. But Tommie wasn't working that much, and she never missed one."

Business. That led to another question. "Did you ever date her?"

"Date? I took her out a time or two for drinks. I do that with most of the girls."

"You're married?"

"Hell, no. Who needs to be married these days?"

"You mean with all the models around?"

"No, man. I keep things strictly professional. I don't mess with the customers. Like, some photogs take what they can get—fringe benefits, say. But they don't last long in this business. Either the customers pay in trade instead of cash, or the good models drop you. Top models don't have to put up with that kind of stuff, man. I've seen it happen."

"But you do go out with them."

"That's rap time—we talk to each other, get into each other's vibes a little. That helps in front of the camera; if I know a little about them, I can help them unlax."

"Was Miss Crowell relaxed?"

"Not right off. I mean, that was her big problem, and this rip-off place she went to didn't do a thing for her. I'd ask for a pose, and it was like she was reading it line by line. It was a real effort for her, she was trying so hard, like. That's why we'd go out for a drink and shoot the shit awhile; when we came back, she could really get it on."

"Do you know if she ever visited the Botanic Gardens?"

The pink glow of Bennett's face turned aside as he thought. "She never said so. I don't remember that she said so."

"Did she talk about boyfriends or people she knew?"

126

The cap of hair glinted as he shook his head. "There's not much time for talking when you work. Sometimes we rapped about her agent."

"What about her agent?"

"Well, that was another thing the modeling school screwed her on. They handed out this crap about placing her with a top agency and then steered her to Jeri Roberts, who just happens to be a partner in the school, and who just happens to be lining up a stable of her own."

"What's wrong with her?"

"It's a new agency. Jeri doesn't have any ins. This town's not the fashion center of the world, man, and there's only so much action to go around. The established places have the big accounts pretty well sewed up."

"What's the agency's name?"

"New Faces. As a matter of fact, Tommie was talking about getting out of her contract. She was getting a lot of free-lance calls and Jeri didn't do a damn thing except take 10 percent off the top." Bennett tested a corner of the film strips with his finger and then washed his hands in the large sink centered on the bench. "I got to print now. These are due first thing tomorrow, and when I print, I concentrate— alone." He turned on a radio adjusted to the wailing of a rhythm-and-blues station.

"Do you know the name of the modeling school Miss Crowell went to?"

"Who doesn't? Famous Faces. They should call it Two Faces."

It was too late to go by the conservatory, and neither the modeling school nor the agency answered Wager's telephone call. The first number just rang; the second had an answering device with a throaty voice that thanked him very much for calling and asked him to leave his message at the sound of the beep. Wager did not leave a message; instead, he lay on his bed in the dark and tried to stifle his restless thoughts until the snap of the clock radio told him it was 10:30. He swung his feet to the floor and rubbed at eyes puffy from the effort to sleep. Pouring a cup of coffee from the pot that stood on its warming plate in the small kitchen, he once more leafed through the little notebook, half aware of the night's silence beginning to settle over the broad, shallow bowl that cradled Denver and its wide belt of suburbs. Rebecca Jean Crowell—Tommie Lee. Like connecting the dots in one of those children's games, gradually an outline, a shape without depth; then, from one angle and another, the slow sketching of shadows and highlights. Tommie Lee—Rebecca Jean Crowell. Wager gazed at the glossy photograph of the smiling girl as if the rigid mouth could speak, as if it could give its own perspective. But of course it couldn't. It was, as the bulldog said, a much different kind of police work from the narcotics section. But Wager felt it was also a hell of a lot different from the collection of facts that Doyle or Ross or Devereaux asked for, too. Somehow he had to move beyond those empty facts into the life of the victim and breathe for her, walk for her; somehow he had to speak for the dead person. He stared a long time at the picture, the details from the little book clustering in different patterns and shapes in his mind. But if he had been asked what he was thinking of, he could honestly answer, "Nothing." Because it was not thought, exactly, that filled his head in the silence of the apartment.

Finally aware that his cup was cold, he sighed and added fresh coffee, then carried the cup with him as he dressed. The clock radio's pale green numbers told him that if he hurried, he had time for one stop before reporting to work.

The Café Chanticleer looked like something out of a World War I movie: a French-style farmhouse complete with a tall, narrow barn adjoining and, tilted beside the entry, a two-wheeled cart spilling dried hay. The host smiled through the candlelight and lifted a menu from the stack on the reception stand. *"Oui, m'sieur?* Table for one?" Here and there in small alcoves, couples talked quietly or sat silent over final plates and glasses; a faint shout of male laughter came from a distant banquet room.

"Maybe next time." Wager showed his badge and the photograph. "Can you tell me if this woman's ever been here?"

The man glanced around the foyer, empty this late on a Wednesday, and then tilted the glossy sheet beneath the low bulb on the reception stand. "Very attractive. She does look kind of familiar...." The French accent had disappeared.

Wager read his hesitation. "She's a homicide victim and I'm trying to find out as much as I can about her."

A small wrinkle came and went above the man's

nose. "If she was here, it was quite a while ago."

"About four months? And before that, she came a lot of times?"

The man glanced up with faint surprise, then shrugged; it wasn't his problem. "Yes. Maybe two dozen times over a year or so."

"With the same person?"

"Yes. I suppose you know who it was."

"You tell me."

Another shrug. "Mr. Pitkin. He brings his friends here quite often."

"Did they ever come with anybody else?"

"Mr. Pitkin and one of his friends? Never. He likes that table over there." He discreetly pointed to a dim corner alcove where the glow of a single candle threw two faint shadows on the wall. Only from the kitchen door could anyone tell whom the shadows belonged to.

"Is he there now?"

"No."

"Who's he brought lately?"

"A blonde. A big one with a very nice figure." He handed the photograph back. "You ... don't believe that Mr. Pitkin ... is involved?"

"It's not likely." He could have added his thought that the unlikely often happened.

A sigh of relief. "I'm glad of that."

"Why?"

"He never seemed like somebody who could—well, do something like that. And he's a good customer— not a big tipper, but a steady one. He's never caused a disturbance. A real gentleman."

"How long has he been coming here?"

"Four or five years now."

"With how many different friends?"

"Who keeps count? He has taste, though; they're all *très bonne*."

Ross and Devereaux had gone home by the time Wager reached the homicide office. He glanced at the empty twenty-four-hour board and headed for the police lab where Baird was just putting his coat on a hanger.

"Good God, Wager. Do you live here?"

"I hear you got a report for me."

"Maybe, maybe not. I haven't had time to look yet." He deliberately placed his coat on a rack and went to the file cabinet. "Right. Here's a real nice report and a fat envelope, just for you."

Wager carried them back to his desk like a dog with a bone and started down the itemized lists. He was finishing the section describing the contents of the vacuum bag when knuckles rapped once on the doorframe of the office. A uniformed sergeant leaned in. "You're Gabe Wager, aren't you?"

Wager vaguely remembered the face from somewhere in District 2—maybe the Traffic Division—but he still needed help from the man's name tag: I. Meyer. Beneath that little chrome rectangle was a newer one: Staff Inspection Bureau. It was a two-year assignment that most experienced officers got and few of them liked; the duty was to make certain that fellow cops did their jobs. "Hello, Irv." Wager held out a hand. "Long time."

"I thought that was you, but I wasn't sure. Putting

on a little weight, eh, Gabe?"

He wasn't. But Irv was one of those people who had to say something cute to put themselves at ease.

"The—ah—bulldog asked me to drop by. To see how things are going."

"Why didn't he come himself?" Wager asked.

"He needs his sleep; he's getting old, Gabe, like all of us. And he's got a touch of the flu. There's a lot of that going around."

"What's he want you to snoop at?"

"Hey, nothing like that. Just routine crap—you know how it goes."

Wager knew that it wasn't routine for a captain to ask the S.I.B. to check up on an officer. "He has a reason, Irv. What is it?"

"The reason is he doesn't feel like getting out of bed at one o'clock in the morning. You're on the graveyard shift, you know. Hey, that's pretty good— the graveyard shift of homicide!"

Wager waited.

"Anyway, he just asked me to ask you—very politely, and only because I was coming down here anyway—how things are going on that Crowell case."

Wager thought so. He pointed to the desk top covered with a stack of canceled checks and papers spilled from the laboratory envelope. "The state's getting its money's worth."

"Don't it always. And then some. So I can tell him things are moving O.K.?"

"As smooth as Ex-Lax." His flare of anger faded as quickly as it came; Meyer didn't like the job he had to do. No cop would. "There's fresh coffee in the

132

machine—help yourself."

"I'd like to, but I got to get out and get seen." A pause told Wager he wasn't through yet.

"What the hell else did Doyle want?"

"Ah—he wanted me to tell you—very politely—that if the case was hung up, not to waste much time on it. Your new partner's due back on the fifth of November, and—ah—the bulldog thought maybe since nothing's turned up yet, you might file the case until you get a little—ah—help."

Wager held himself rigid against the desk. "That's very thoughtful of him, Irv. I'll do my best not to catch the killer."

"Doyle didn't mean it that way!" Meyer rubbed at the hairline far beneath his hat. "He was just a little worried that maybe you might waste time on this when you're needed on the street. Or maybe get in too much of a hurry and use some procedures that were—ah—unorthodox. You know how he feels about narcotics procedures."

"I'm not in narcotics. I'm in homicide."

"I know that! But the bulldog—well . . ."

"He has already told me, Irv. Twice."

"All I'm doing is my job, all right?" It was Meyer's turn to get pissed because he didn't like what the bulldog made him do, and if Wager had not been an ex-narc, he wouldn't be doing it.

"Fine. And I'll do mine. Sergeant," said Wager.

"Fine. Detective."

The S.I.B. man's heels smacked against the tiles of the hallway.

Screw Doyle and Meyer both. Wager couldn't decide which he disliked more, Doyle's nervousness about his narcotics background, or Meyer's pussyfooted way of trying to do a job. Screw both of them. He sipped once at his coffee to burn out the bilious taste of his anger and then turned back to the papers on his desk.

The canceled checks were in numerical order, beginning with number 237 and dated January 2, 1976. It was to Conoco Oil Company for $14.19. He leafed through the slips, noting a monthly payment to Famous Faces for $50, occasional payments to High Country Profiles ranging from $26.23 to $131.11. He counted five of those checks, the last dated in September. Other payments were for rent, for "cash"—usually in twenty-dollar amounts—to King Soopers or Safeway, to half a dozen department or clothing stores. Something about those store names—something half familiar in those names; Wager thumbed through the appointment book that was becoming as well known to him as his own notebook. There: three sets of initials that fit three of the names on the checks—"A.I.," Ardree Innis; "F.W.," Fashion Wear; "E," Emporium. The only Ardree Innis in the telephone book was a boldface entry repeated in the yellow pages: "Exquisite Fashions for Women."

Wager counted the cryptic entries in the Crowell appointment book. At first they came one or two a week, then toward November as many as six, sometimes two or three a day. Fashion shows! Somewhere along the way, he had read the initials as men's names, and to find out that they weren't made him feel curiously better and worse—better about the name of the victim, worse about losing a possible lead on who killed her.

He dug through the canceled checks for the returned deposit slips and monthly statements. Seldom did she leave more than $100 in the bank at the end of a month, though the September statement noted a balance of $114.51. If the fashion shows brought enough money, then she covered her known expenses—without blackmailing, without whoring. And still without a motive for getting killed.

Turning to the other papers in the small stack, he found the title to her car, the 1976 license number matching the number of his notebook; a call to the Traffic Division told him what he suspected—that the car had not yet been spotted.

Beneath a collection of assorted receipts lay a letter from her parents tucked into an opened envelope. Among the lines of pale blue ink, erect parentheses singled out items that might have been answered. Wager hoped so, because the parentheses brought into focus the image that he had been forming: that the girl ordered her life as straight as a ruled line to whatever goal she wanted. She was dedicated, orderly, persistent. Wager liked those traits. And she had an honesty he could understand, too; Pitkin had brought that out. Yet somehow she carried those traits to someone who had not liked them—someone who hated them enough to kill her. That someone murdered her not for any apparent threat she might hold, but simply because she wasn't what the killer wanted her to be.

Wager's pencil tapped gently but insistently on the

fiber blotter that held the little stack of papers. There was something like motive. A crazy one, maybe, and no factual evidence led to it. Nowhere in Doyle's procedure manual would Wager find support for the feeling. And even if he located a suspect, he sure as hell couldn't get near a courtroom with just that feeling. But it lay there in his mind like a stone under sand—he could feel it in those hazy thoughts, if they could be called thoughts. It was there: a growing sense of what the murderer was like because he was beginning to know what the victim was like. Just as he had seen in his mind's eye the shadowy figure squat in the dark conservatory to stare at the head, so now he could almost name the motive, almost say what would make someone kill this girl.

"Any homicide detective." His radio woke him to the two-toned wall of the office. "Any homicide detective."

"X-eighty-five."

"We have a ten-thirty-one in the alley behind 1706 East Colfax. Shots have been fired; squad in vicinity."

Crime in progress. Always something in progress—he wouldn't put it past Doyle to set up some action just to make sure Wager was on the street. "Ten-Four."

Quickly gathering the papers, he slipped them into the laboratory envelope, pausing when one near the bottom caught his eye. It was a light tan brochure that opened into eight panels and described the history and holdings of the Denver Botanic Gardens.

11

His alarm buzzed at 1:30 P.M. and his hand groped
for the snooze button, then stopped as he remembered: Thursday—one day less. Usually, the faint
click of the radio woke him to turn off the station
before his mind was invaded by the insistent drawling
voice of the afternoon disk jockey with its heavy
struggle to be witty, persuasive, and hip. There were
better radio stations, but none that woke him more
quickly; and when two minutes of that voice failed its
duty, the buzzer sounded. Today's was third-degree
weariness, and he began to think that the eight-to-
four shift next month would seem like a vacation.
Maybe Ross was right about letting the case work itself
out. For the night shift, anyway. His hand slid over
the pillow with its lingering spot of warmth. To hell
with Ross—cases didn't work themselves out; someone had to work them. He stumped into the kitchen
to start the pot of coffee and chop onions and sausage
for a Marine Corps omelette.

While he ate, he laid out the four hours left in the
normal working day: first, Crowell's last known job—
the modeling agency; then, the Botanic Gardens—
that damned key, and now a brochure that said she
might have visited it while she was alive. He made the
first call after stacking the dishes in a dishwasher that
had been too small for Lorraine but was the right size
for one user.

"New Faces Modeling Agency!"

"I'd like to talk to Miss Jeri Roberts, please."

"I'll see if she's in! Who may I say is calling?"

"Detective Gabriel Wager of the Denver Police Department."

"Oh! One moment, please!"

It was more than a moment, but worth it to clear his ear of hot, breathless eagerness. "This is Jeri Roberts."

Wager identified himself again. "I'd like to talk with you about a girl who worked for you—Miss Rebecca Jean Crowell. She also used the name Tommie Lee."

"Oh, yes. I saw that in the paper this morning. It's awful."

Denver's morning paper was the *Rocky Mountain News*; Gargan's paper, the *Post,* was an afternoon sheet. Some rival had beat him to the story, and Wager couldn't help a tiny smile. "Are you free now? Can I come over?"

"Certainly."

The office wasn't what Wager expected; he imagined that modeling agencies featured shiny chrome-and-glass rooms with furniture somehow shaped like the smoothly curved letters seen in mod advertisements. Instead, the New Faces Agency was in a converted two-story home on East Eighth Avenue, complete with lace curtains and a fireplace that held the marks of real soot. The receptionist's desk was just inside the entry.

"Hello! You must be the detective!"

"Yes, ma'am." He was relieved that he didn't look like a male model, then wondered why it was so easy to tell he was a detective.

138

"Wow! Have a seat! I'll tell Miss Roberts you're here!"

He wandered into the living room and stared at the wall of pictures filled with posturing men, women, and children. Behind him, the receptionist pushed a button on an intercom and breathed, "He's here!"

A door opened and a short woman with cropped black hair strode out quickly; she shook hands like a man. "I'm Jeri Roberts. Come in the office." It was not an invitation.

She stood beside one of the old-fashioned floor-to-ceiling windows with her back to Wager and stared at the dark red of the brick wall next door. Then she blew her nose and took three quick steps to the desk. A jerking movement thumped a bottle of Jim Beam Green Label on the littered desk. "Sit down. Drink?"

"No, thanks." Wager had bought the *News* on the way over. The brief article identified Rebecca Jean Crowell and said that last week her body had been found in one place, her head in another. It did not mention Tommie Lee or the New Faces Agency.

She poured a three-finger drink into a tumbler and splashed a touch of water on top of it. In two gulps, it was gone. "You wanted to ask questions." Most people would have explained a drink like that: the death was such a shock, Rebecca was such a dear friend. But Miss Roberts only poured another one and squeaked the cork into the bottle. "Go ahead."

"How long did you know Miss Crowell?"

She leaned back in the swivel chair and lifted down a thin volume from a short bookshelf filled with similar black bindings. Each had a name in gold leaf on the spine. The first page gave the information: "Since August 8, 1975. She enrolled with my affiliate, the Famous Faces Modeling School on that date. She had her first employment for us in February of this year."

"How long has she used the name Tommie Lee?"

"Since we put her file together," a rapid peck on the book with a blunt fingernail. "'Crowell' just didn't have it, and 'Rebecca' sounded too Jewish." Wager thought that he hid surprise, but she caught it. "A number of our customers equate Jewishness with New York. That works against a local model unless she's top of the line. They like to think we have enough local talent."

"Don't we?"

"Some of the boys are all right. But local girls move like cows. Most of my girls come from somewhere else."

"I thought the model stood still for pictures and such."

"Pictures? Photography? There's not much in that line out here yet. The local money's still in fashion shows."

"She did a lot of those?"

"As many as I could book her for."

"Was she good at it?"

"Not very. But she was one of my hardest workers and getting a little better all the time."

"So she could make a living at it?"

"Not a good one. Cigarette?" Wager said no; Roberts waved the match out with a snap of her wrist. "Goddamned few models make a good living in this town. If you want to make it as a model, you go to

Chicago or San Francisco or New York. Especially New York."

"Was that Miss Crowell's plan?"

"That was her plan, yes."

"But?"

The small head gave a sharp shake. "She'd never make it there. I told her that."

"Why not?"

"By the time she learned what so many others were born with, she'd be too old. Hell, she was twenty-three already."

"I heard that more than anything in the world, she wanted to be a model."

"Most people don't get what they want more than anything in the world." The cork squeaked out of the bottle. "I think perhaps Rebecca was a little insane on the subject. It happens."

"What did she say when you told her that?"

"Nothing. She simply didn't believe me. I said she'd be better off in Denver doing local stuff because the competition could chew her up anywhere else. You have to understand, Mr. Wager, this is one very tough business."

He believed her. "According to her appointment book, she had more and more fashion shows."

"Yes—the advance shows for spring begin as early as October. Then comes the Christmas business— retail customers—which starts around Thanksgiving. She was getting her share of that, and there's some money in it around here. But in a bigger city she'd have been squeezed out of that market, too." The head shook once. "She just did not believe me."

"How much did she make?"

Miss Roberts turned another page or two. "On a good day, she got sixty dollars. That's three shows at twenty dollars each—standard rate for an inexperienced model. Out of that, she had to pay her own transportation and other expenses."

The most shows in a week that Wager had counted in the appointment book was twelve—$240 for a good week, and there had been a number of poor ones. "Do you have a lot of people who want to be models?" The question was more for himself than for Rebecca Crowell.

"Hundreds, Mr. Wager. Hundreds 'right here in River City.'" A small, hard smile widened the corners of her mouth, and Wager half wondered if at times his own mouth looked that way; it was the faint smile of satisfaction at seeing someone get the trouble they deserved. "Every woman between thirteen and thirty-three, and, any more, most of the men."

"Have you been an agent very long?"

"Too damned long for my health. I was an executive director in a New York agency until two sons of bitches ganged up to push me out. I came here four years ago to start all over."

"And you're doing O.K.?"

"You are goddamned right I am."

He'd heard that phrase recently; he'd heard it from Lisa Dahl, who was also starting all over. And it struck his ear with the same slightly hollow sound as if Jeri Roberts, like Miss Dahl, found that the only difference between the new start and the old was that now she could see her mistakes coming—that nothing really changed for the better. But you either kept trying or you died. It was something that Rebecca Crowell might have learned, too, before she died. "Do you recognize any of these initials or names?" He handed her a slip of paper listing the brief entries from the appointment book. "They might have to do with the modeling business. Some of the initials are maybe store names."

She settled a pair of large horn-rimmed glasses on her nose. "Yes." She gave names to the initials; Wager had guessed right on three. "But these first names could be anyone." The glasses jerked up. "These are Rebecca's notes?"

"Yes."

"Then 'Phil' must be that whimp of a photographer who was trying to take every cent she made—Phil Bennett."

"I thought models needed pictures to show customers?"

"You've been talking to him. The only models who need that many pictures are TV and publications models. Girls like Rebecca who work fashion shows do most of their advertising live. Local buyers see them at work and hire them for their own shows. The out-of-town trade comes through me. Most salespeople from out of town don't see the models until the show. That's what agents are for."

"She missed a lot of these shows after she was killed. Didn't you worry about where she might be?"

"I was worried that she wasn't where she was supposed to be. That's all. It happens all the time—girls come and go; and while it surprised me that someone like Rebecca missed the shows, it's just not that unusual." She sighed and added, "I did call a couple of times. There was no answer, of course. So I figured, screw her."

"Do you know if she ever went to the Botanic Gardens?"

"Damned if I know. I didn't know this burg even had any until I read about where they found her."

"Did she have any boyfriends that you heard about?"

"You mean like 'Ralph' or 'Allen,' here?"

"Them or anybody else."

"Most of the girls have husbands or boyfriends. Some have both, some have more than one of each. But Rebecca never talked about these two or anyone else. She was strictly business." Miss Roberts gazed out the window again. "It really is too bad."

"What is?"

"Rebecca had the right attitude to make it in this business—she'd cut her mother's throat. . . . I guess I shouldn't have said it, but that's the kind of insanity it takes. Total dedication, and to hell with everybody else."

Total dedication did not sound like insanity to Wager. "Was she scheduled for a show tonight?"

Another glance at the file. "Yes. The Jetliner Motel."

"Motel?"

"A promotion stunt for a convention. Motel convention directors like to have cocktail-hour shows for the visitors' wives. No one ever buys a thing, but it's a cheap way for dress stores to get known, and it makes the convention a little classier. Besides, I will take

144

every bit of business I can get—from anywhere!"
That slight stretch of the mouth was somewhere between a faint smile and a set of the jaw. "And I've
already lined up a replacement for Tommie Lee."

The Botanic Gardens was a short drive from the
New Faces Agency. At this time of day, the narrow
parking lot was half filled, though only a few people
strolled outside in the broad spaces that were now
brown and empty of plants. It was one of those late-
autumn afternoons when cloudless skies held a hot
sun and cold air—one of those bright days when, as
his grandfather used to say, the sun had a bite to it. A
hard wind blew away the city's smog and brought the
snow-dusted mountains so close that Wager could see
the blue dots of pine trees scattered along their
flanks. He gave himself a few quiet minutes in a sheltered corner of the concrete walls to feel the sun burn
against his face and the cloth of his trousers and coat.
Then he went looking for Mr. Sumner.
He found him talking with a round-shouldered
man in a green wool blazer, and at first, Mr. Sumner
did not remember Wager's face. "Oh—you're the
police officer!"
"Yes, sir. I wonder if you've ever seen this woman
here before?"
Sumner frowned at the photograph. "Not to my
knowledge. Of course, we have so many people passing through." He looked up. "I take it this is the
victim?"
"We identified her yesterday as Rebecca Jean
Crowell."

The name meant nothing to Sumner. He shook his head. "Poor thing. Mr. Weimer and I were just discussing some kind of special display that would take people's minds off what happened."

The round-shouldered man touched Wager's fingers in a cautious handshake. "Most of our recent visitors haven't come just to see our specimens, I'm afraid."

"And it's quite bothersome for those who have. It's difficult to realize just how macabre people can be." Sumner handed the photograph to Weimer.

"This seems to be a professional pose," he said.

"She was a model," said Wager. "She was also called Tommie Lee."

"Well, she certainly did not do any posing here!" Sumner glared around the lobby echoing with the clatter of footsteps and voices that ran together in a buzz beneath the sound of the reflecting pool fountain.

"I thought you let photographers in."

"Amateurs only. And then absolutely no artificial lighting—flash bulbs or otherwise. None. Specimens have been damaged in the past by heat and by exploding bulbs. And naturally we do not want the pathways blocked by all the equipment that professionals bring with them. No, if she came here, it wasn't as a model. Absolutely forbidden. We have a sign. Right there!" He pointed to the wall.

Wager turned to Weimer. "You were at a convention in St. Louis on the nineteenth?"

"Yes. I was back there when it happened."

"Did you have your key to the conservatory with

146

you?"

"My key?" His brown eyes widened. "Of course— it's on the same ring as my house and car keys. It's always with me." He pulled out a ring with a green rubber leaf for a tag. "See?"

He saw. "Do you mind if I show this picture to some of the workers, Mr. Sumner?"

Sumner didn't. Wager wandered among the clusters of people drifting down the gritty paths until he found Solano. The utility worker stepped to the middle of the path to peer at the photograph and then shook his head slowly. "She sure don't look like what I found." The man spoke very loudly and a group of people stopped to listen. "When I found it, I'd of never guessed she looked that good, Officer."

"Pardon me, young man." An old lady bent like a hairpin tugged at Solano's denim shirt. "Are you the one who found that head?"

"Yes, ma'am. I was just coming on work, just up there by the big waterfall, and I just felt something was wrong. Even before I saw anything, I just knew deep down *something* was right over there in the dark, lurking. . . ."

Wager went in search of Mauro.

The thick-bodied man was in Greenhouse 1 loading trays of asters onto a long worktable. He gave the picture a quick glance. "Nope. Never saw her before."

Wager studied Mauro's face, with its realigned nose and the carefully distant eyes that tried to hide the man's feelings about cops. "You didn't take a real good look."

"It's good enough to tell."

"You're sure?"

"I'm sure."

"Mauro, you did some time a while back for being dumb. I hope you're smart enough now to tell me the truth."

"You checked me out?"

"Sure. Every citizen at the scene of a crime gets checked out. That's democracy in action."

"Well, screw you, fuzz. These people know about my record. And they know I've been clean ever since."

"The girl's name was Rebecca Jean Crowell or Tommie Lee. She was twenty-three, a model, and her parents will be burying her in a sealed box." He held out the photograph again. "And you better be goddamned sure about what you tell me."

One of Mauro's thick hands pulled the photograph close to his bent nose and he squinted for a very long time; then he slowly looked Wager in the eyes. "I never seen her before."

Mauro was lying. Wager knew it absolutely.

He was unlocking his car when a familiar voice called across the parking lot, "Wager—hey! Hold on!"

Gargan sprinted from a brown sedan that bore black-and-white press plates under the Colorado license. "Man—it's hotter than hell today." A finger dug at the knit collar of his black turtleneck. "For a working man, anyhow. You look your usual cool self."

"That comes from taking siestas."

"I'll have to try that. What's new on the Crowell thing?"

"About the same as before. How about you?"

"Me? Gabe Wager, El Supercop and loping lone wolf, is asking this humble reporter what he has?"

"I heard you were the *Daily Planet*'s ace reporter—or some word like 'ace.'"

Gargan raised his eyebrows in wonder. "You just tried to make a funny, Wager. I hardly recognize this nimble-witted new you. But as a matter of fact, El Supremo, I do have something." He waited until Wager gave in.

"What?"

"You really didn't want to ask that, did you?" Gargan laughed and jabbed a finger at Wager's chest. "You almost choked before you could ask that, didn't you?"

He wondered if drinking printer's ink kept a lot of reporters from growing up. "What is it, Gargan?"

"The victim was a model for the New Faces Agency—when I finish interviewing Solano, I'll be going over there." He grinned. "You can come along if you like and learn how information's gathered."

It wasn't the "what" but the "how" that interested Wager. "Where'd you get your information?"

"Process of deduction, my dear flatfoot. Besides, I got a buddy who knows all about the modeling game."

"He knew Crowell?"

"Down, boy, down! No, he didn't know her. But he told me how to find out who she worked for."

"How?"

Gargan winked. "That's privileged information. First Amendment guarantees."

"Who is this friend?"

"You're going to ask him about New Faces? You don't take my word for it?"

"I'm going to ask him if he really calls himself your friend. What's his name?"

"Oh, you're cute. But I'll lay a deal on you—I'll tell you his name if you tell me what you're doing here."

"O.K." It was Wager's turn to wait; if Gargan wanted to play games, Wager would beat him at his game.

"Me first, right? You trusting s.o.b. He's Saul Kramer—Kramer Studios over on fifteenth. Used to work for the *Post* and then went free-lance. Now, give!"

"What are you doing here?" Wager asked.

"That's *my* question!"

Wager shrugged. "All or nothing."

Gargan shook his head. "I'll bet you cheat at solitaire, too. My editor gave me the O.K. to do an indepth on this one; the wire services are still interested. I'm here to get the unvarnished impressions of the guy who found the head."

"Solano'll be happy to tell you all about it."

"Jesus, I'm glad to hear that. I talked to that bastard Sumner on the telephone and he was scared shitless to let me near the place. 'Absolutely no photographs,' he said. I told him he'd get a hell of a lot of bad publicity if he didn't let me do my job. We servants of the fourth estate are not without power! Your turn."

"Identification." He showed Gargan the picture of Crowell.

"Hey, that's nice stuff. Was nice stuff. Too bad. Can I have this? You got another copy?"

150

"No and no. But give the mortuary a call and see what the arrangements are. If the parents are coming to pick up the pieces, Gargan, maybe you can have some fun with them."

The reporter finally got angry. "That's a shitty thing to say, Wager." Then he thought a moment. "But it's a good story angle. Thanks."

Wager started his car and rolled down his window. "Gargan—give my regards to Jeri Roberts."

"Who's that?"

"She owns New Faces."

His last glimpse of the reporter was in the rear-view mirror; the man's mouth was still open.

There was no "Saul" in Crowell's appointment book, and this would be another long shot; but, short or long, the shots had to be taken. And it was a way of filling time until he could act on the more important thing in the back of his mind. Much of a cop's life was filling in time, living in a car with grimy floor mats and scraps of official forms, ashtrays packed with someone else's stale cigarette butts, air moist with the breath of whoever drove the car earlier. It all brought that familiar sense of swimming in a river crowded with other swimmers—river and swimmers both invisible to John Q. Citizen. And though Wager didn't like much about it, it was home and he spent a lot of life there.

Yet this case made even those familiar things and smells seem awry, somehow. Maybe it was just being on the night shift; he hoped that the next nighttime victim was a nighttime person; then maybe things would fit a little better. Because there would be another victim. Always another victim, and Wager saw why Ross and Devereaux were in no hurry when there were no immediate witnesses.

He threaded among the downtown traffic of 15th Street and pulled into a no-parking zone, flipping down the sun visor with its "Police Car" tag. Maybe it was the worrisome feeling of something solid just out of sight that, with a little more reaching, a little more grabbing, he should get hold of. But it had not happened yet. It was just there, just beyond reach, but it had not happened yet.

Kramer Studios was a long, narrow shop wedged between a topless bar and one of the few mom-and-pop grocery stores still alive in Denver. Down one side ran a long glass case full of sample frames and photographs; facing it was a maroon expanse of velvet wallpaper checkered with framed pictures of all sizes. A balding man in his late forties pushed through a black curtain at the far end; Wager might have remembered him from the *Post*.

"Yes, sir?"

"I'm Detective Wager, D.P.D. Maybe you can help me with a case I'm working on."

"Wager? Yeah—I thought you looked familiar. Is this another narc bust?" He held out a hand.

They shook hands. "Homicide. Gargan tells me you know a lot about the modeling business."

"A lot? No, I know some photographers who specialize in that end of the business, but I'm mostly a portrait man myself. Wedding, family, that sort of thing."

152

Wager was puzzled. "But Gargan said you knew the agency Rebecca Crowell worked for."

"I'd never heard of her. All I told him was to call the agencies in the yellow pages and ask. Hell, there's only five or six listed; it's no real chore. They all keep records of their models."

Wager tried not to grin at himself; it would take too long to explain to Kramer, and he probably wouldn't see what was funny anyway. "Do you know a Phil Bennett of High Country Profiles?"

"Phil? Sure. He does a lot of work with models."

"He's a good fashion photographer?"

"I guess so. But I wouldn't call him a fashion photographer. He mostly does portfolio work. I suppose he could do more that was straight advertising and commercial stuff—God knows the business is starting to grow. But he gets his kicks out of training the girls."

"Training them?"

"Yeah. For camera work. He tells me there's no modeling school in town that really teaches people how to act in front of a camera. He really gets ticked off at that."

"Is he good at this training?"

"I guess. There's people around who knock him for his prices and think he's just trying to sell pictures. Hell, selling pictures is the name of the game. But I heard of a couple girls who moved on to bigger and better things because of what he taught them."

"Who?"

"Names? I can't give you names. I just heard one works full time for Sears—she's been in every catalogue for the last three years. Phil told me the other went to San Francisco about a year ago and is doing real well."

"How is he with male models?"

"He only handles women." Kramer saw Wager's expression. "There's nothing wrong with that—some shooters specialize in women, others in kids, others in old folks. And then you've got the rocks-and-trees people and some who do only pet portraits. Phil's lucky enough to pick a subject that gives him a living and a little excitement, too."

"Have you ever seen this girl before?"

Kramer looked at it and then glanced at the credit on the back. "Phil's work. I thought so—he's good at taking out shadow. Me, I like a little for contrast and highlight." He pointed to one of the wedding pictures in the glass case. "No, I've never seen her. This is the girl who was killed? The one who had her head cut off?"

"Yes."

"That's really awful. She's a very pretty girl—a good subject. It's awful that somebody would kill her and then do something like that. The guy who did it must be a maniac."

"We'll find out," said Wager.

But even insanity has its own structure, Wager told himself as one more time he drove through the downtown streets and swung past the chocolate-colored block of the Brown Palace Hotel. The evidence pointed to an acquaintance of the girl—to more than that, to someone who could get within arm's reach while carrying a butcher knife. To someone who had a key to the conservatory. Maybe to someone who lied about knowing her.

There were constants in all this: a friend, a place, an opportunity, a motive. Perhaps the motive was insane, but it had its own logic. That logic was seen in the mutilation and careful placing of the head and body. And that was linked to another constant: Rebecca herself.

Wager parked a half-block from the domed flash of the conservatory at an angle that let him watch the employee door. Solano's red Toyota with its white camper shell had already left—probably for the afternoon papers to see if his interview was in it yet. In a little while, a car full of groundskeepers backed out and drove up the short alley past him. Wager waited. He wasn't hungry, but he wished for the thermos of coffee that he usually propped on the seat beside him during surveillance. Finally, a bit after five, he recognized Mauro's heavy shape—the last to leave—bend over the latch of the door and then step back to give it a hard shake before turning away. On the map in his mind, Wager drew a little line between the Botanic Gardens and Mauro's home; he let the utility worker arc out of sight down a narrow street littered with brown leaves shoaling and skittering in the strong wind. Then he started the car and drove parallel to that imaginary line and waited at the next intersection. In two or three minutes, Mauro crossed at the traffic light a block away. Wager coasted slowly to the next intersection to wait again.

Mauro had lied about recognizing the girl; Wager

smelled that odor about the man as sharp as cat shit. He'd never really wondered why, but it was a fact; it was easier to know when an ex-con blew smoke than when a lot of straights did. Maybe Wager just spoke the ex-con's language better. Or maybe the odds favored an ex-con lying to a cop. Either way, he knew Mauro had lied. And he knew Mauro had a key to the conservatory.

The worker didn't show at the next crossing. Wager turned quickly through the light traffic and down the block. Halfway along the street Mauro had traveled was a neighborhood tavern: Elton's Place. From its façade, Wager knew the kind of bar it was—small, the owner himself behind the cash register, dried beef strips and pickled pig's knuckles and boiled eggs waiting, the customers a few regulars who found a home where they could watch television and buy enough beer to keep the place going. He parked and set the rear-view mirror to watch the tavern's doorway. A half-hour later, Mauro came out; Wager followed the shape in the glass as it walked with that slightly waddling step that some heavy-legged men have. Looping around the block, Wager trailed Mauro the eight more streets to his home, a house with a steep, English-looking roof and a pointed front door. The yard was filled with carefully tended shrubs and clumps of birch and large spruce. Wager let Mauro disappear inside the house and cruised past to fix it in memory; then he looked for a telephone.

The bulldog himself answered. "What are you doing on duty, Wager?"

"I'm not. But there are some things I want to look

156

into, and everybody's asleep when I'm working."

Doyle didn't know whether to be pleased at Wager's dedication or worried about him being a prima donna. "What things?"

"I need some information on one Dominick G. Mauro. Residence, 1308 Garfield; his place of work is the Botanic Gardens."

"What's he done to deserve this honor?"

"He has a jacket." Which was enough for most cops, Wager included. "And he wasn't at work during the twenty-four-hour period when Crowell was killed and dumped."

"Where was he?"

The bulldog sure went to the heart of things. "I don't know, Captain. That's what I want to find out. I'm hoping that somebody can talk to his landlord and see if he was home from, say, 9 A.M. to 3 P.M. on October 19th."

"All right." A pause while the man on the other end wrote down the information needed. "Is he home now? What time's he go to work?"

"It should be clear any time after eleven in the morning."

"I'll send somebody over tomorrow. Anything else?"

"No, sir."

12

Though Wager had seen the Jetliner Motel count-
less times, he'd never been there; it was one of the
kind that blended into the tangle of businesses along
every highway through Denver. Some twenty blocks
west of Stapleton International on Smith Road, it was
a convenient taxi ride from the airport and visible but
hard to get to from I-70. Its yellow neon airplane rose
in the night sky above lesser marquees and signs beside the bumpy road, and to judge from the neighboring ranks of tractor-trailers, small ill-lit bars,
warehouses, and cattle-loading docks, the motel had
most of its trade from truckers and visitors to the
National Western Stock Show. Wager parked just beyond the A-frame that tried to make the entry look
impressive. Through the glass wall at the back of the
lobby, he saw a large court of two-story units surrounding a pool. Small wisps of steam rose from the
glowing water, but no one was swimming. In the
lobby, the ashtrays overflowed onto the orange carpet, and here and there in the short pile, heel marks
of old mud aimed at the reception desk. It wasn't the
kind of place Wager associated with either conven-
tions or fashion shows, but a letter board welcomed
members of the A.A.A.I and told them to please register here.

"What's the A.A.A.I?" Wager asked the clerk.

The slim young man looked as if his feet had been

nailed to the floor two days ago. He answered without a smile, "American Association of Artificial Inseminators."

"They're having the convention?"

"The regional arm is."

An arm of the Artificial Inseminators Association? Wager looked to see if the young man was joking, but the gray face was blank.

"Do you want a room?" he asked Wager.

"No. I was told there's a fashion show here tonight."

The tired face finally showed a quiver of life. "You're interested in fashions?"

"Something wrong with that?"

A weary shrug; he saw all kinds on the night shift. "In the Jetliner Lounge. Just around there."

It was too dark to tell if the lounge was as ill-kept as the lobby. A purple neon tube ran atop the mirror behind the bar and gave a little glow, but most of the light on that side of the room splashed up from the working area beneath the bar. A scattering of orange candle glasses marked tables drifting out to the left; and Wager made out a line of silhouettes sitting on barstools and the pale reflection of clothes and flesh at the dark tables. In the center of the ceiling hung a model 747 with glowing portholes. He groped his way to a vinyl chair that felt sticky and rose no higher than the small of his back.

"Yes, sir?" The waitress wore something like the upper half of a stewardess uniform.

"Is this where they have the fashion show?" He saw no stage, none of the runways or platforms that, from newspaper pictures, he thought fashion shows needed.

"Yes, sir. The girls will be on at seven o'clock. What do you want to drink?"

"Just a draw."

She faded into the darkness. Slowly, Wager began to see faces and shapes grouped in the glow of candlelight. At a very tiny table against one wall, Jeri Roberts talked to another woman, who also had cropped hair. Her lips moved rapidly and she leaned forward tensely as if the stream of words needed pushing. He would speak with Roberts later; right now, he just wanted to sit and look and feel—to see the place as Rebecca Crowell might have seen it, or as somebody might have seen her in it.

Plastic tags that said "Hello! I'm——" glinted here and there on men's coats; the women at those tables were wives. A few talked to each other with wagging hands and nervous laughter; most tried to make their husbands think they weren't bored—after all, they'd wanted to come along. At other tables, men wearing open shirts, short hair, and cowboy boots looked as if they would feel more at home on the barstools— except that other men like them were already there: truck drivers whose lines booked them overnight at the Jetliner. Here and there, in the darker corners, sat a few men alone like Wager. Like Mauro might have sat. Wager was very interested in them.

His second beer was losing its chill when three slender, overdressed women clustered in the bright hall just outside the doorway. They took a deep breath, then blew in with a graceful sway that, in its own way, was as out of place as the awkward truck drivers hunched over the tiny tables. The three spread through the room to pause like butterflies at each table and to smile and spin around and say something that Wager couldn't quite hear over the talk and laughter and television noises from the bar. One of the wives at the next table reached to finger the transparent cape of a dress and Wager thought he caught the word "washable." Then a light swirl of cloth brushed near his arm.

"Hi—this evening we're showing Ardree Innis's spring fashions. This number follows the peasant styling so popular this season. It's cotton plissé accentuated with a fringed sash. The skirt and bodice can be worn together or separately." The tall girl with short blond hair smiled widely and spun once to make the long dress flare out in a restless shimmer of flowered patterns. Then she stood still for a count of three.

She had very small breasts, he thought. "Yes, ma'am."

"It costs eighty-nine ninety-five and comes in all sizes. The Ardree Innis store is located at 1601 South Broadway, and their spring fashion preview will be held tomorrow at 2 P.M."

"Yes, ma'am."

She left a calling card on the edge of the table and spun away. It said "Ardree Innis Exquisite Fashions" and repeated the address. Wager watched the thin ankles twinkle to a halt at the truck drivers' table, and he wondered how the girl could smile that widely and talk at the same time.

"Boy, howdy!" The skinniest of the truck drivers grinned up at the girl. "I don't know much about dresses, but you sure are something. How much for you?"

The blonde kept smiling. "Only the dress is for sale." She quickly floated to the next table.

The truck driver hopped up to call after her, "I'll buy it! Right now! Take it off!" He sank back, giggling under the laughing thumps of one of his buddies.

Suddenly the waitresses started their rounds and the models were gone.

"Is it all over?" he asked the girl in half a uniform.

"Oh, no. They got two more showings. You want another beer or are you going to make that one last?"

In five minutes they were back, this time wearing light-colored suits or shirts and slacks. They moved directly between tables now, spending time at those with conventioneers or where the men nodded and tried to look serious and act as if they knew what to ask about cut or material. Wager again just said "Yes, ma'am," and the girls didn't stay long at his table. When the tall blonde crossed the room, the skinny truck driver stood again. "Hey, girlie, I'll buy that one, too—right now!"

As they finished their round, each passed Jeri Roberts's table; there it was all business—a silent pirouette, no smile, an occasional quick question, and an answer just as terse. He waited until the three models left the room, then took his beer to the Roberts table. "Can I sit here?"

She squinted up. "The detective? What's your name?"

"Wager."

"Wager. Sit down, Wager." She made as much

room as she could at the small formica table and introduced him to the other woman, who said, "Oh, I heard about it! It's one of the worst things I ever heard of in my life!"

Jeri Roberts drank deeply and lit a cigarette; a little blue flame shot up at the cigarette's end and Wager wondered how much whiskey the woman had had since he saw her this afternoon. "Thanks a hell of a lot, Detective Wager."

"For what?"

"For sicking that goddamned reporter on me. This business is tough enough without that kind of publicity."

Wager didn't think of murder as publicity. "What did Gargan tell you?"

"Yeah. Gargan. That was his name. He said you told him Tommie Lee worked for me and that you gave him the go-ahead to do a feature on her."

"He was lying and using my name to make you talk to him. Somebody else told him who she worked for, and I don't have authority to give him a go-ahead on anything."

She weighed his words very deliberately, and Wager figured she had done a lot of drinking since this afternoon. "Oh." Then, "I apologize."

"No offense. Did Miss Crowell do much work in this place?"

"Yes. A lot of the girls don't like it here, so I always need somebody. Tommie—Rebecca—worked whenever I asked her to."

"Why don't they like it?"

Roberts snorted and poked her cigarette at the

table of truck drivers. "The wise-asses. This place has more than its share of wise-asses."

"Do any of these people try to date the girls?"

"Sure. All the time. It's part of the business. But unless they're a customer of the agency, it's a no-no."

"Crowell never got picked up? Maybe by a heavyset man a little bit taller than me?"

"No. She did not."

"None of the girls ever get picked up?"

"It happens. Yes, it does happen every now and then that I end up with a girl who tries to use my shows to advertise her own business. They're the kind that can't type and can't model either. But when I find out about it, they're out on their tail. I'll be god-damned if I let my company turn into a whorehouse. What they do on their own time is one thing, but my shows are strictly business. Strictly!"

"So Crowell never had a date with anybody she met at a show?"

"I've said that. She wasn't the kind I had to worry about."

Wager started to ask another question, but the woman held up her hand like a traffic cop. "Here they come. How long did that change take, honey?"

"Twelve minutes," said the friend.

"Too goddamned long. They lose momentum when they take too long."

The three wore evening clothes this time, long dresses that either clung smoothly to straight, slender hips or swung out into a hem that looked to Wager like the points of a tablecloth hanging down. The one girl with long hair had piled it into a swirl on top of her head, and the skinny truck driver called out, "Oh, man, look at that one!"

"Cindy's still too stiff," said the friend.

"Maybe I should have given her another drink," said Roberts. "But I'm not sure it would help."

"Do they drink before a show?" asked Wager.

"I usually give them just one. To relax them." She showed Wager her taut smile. "Provided they're of age, of course."

"Would Miss Crowell drink?"

"Yes." Her attention was on the girls. "There— that's a good turn. If only she'd remember to show the clothes instead of herself." Roberts waited until the girl with long hair glided near the table: "Cindy, dear!"

"Yes, Jeri"

"Take a moment to hold the dress out. Let the customers see the fabric."

"All right." She poised at a conventioneers' table and lifted one side of the dress.

"Did Crowell work on the morning of Tuesday, October 19th?"

Roberts frowned. "Jesus, that was nine days ago. Who can remember? We do a few morning shows— call the secretary tomorrow. She'll have a record of anything Rebecca was paid for."

"Are these three girls in the Famous Faces School?"

"Only Cindy."

"Are they all full-time models?"

"Julie is." Roberts nodded toward the blonde. "And she works her tail off at it. She has herself and a daughter to support. Ann's a part-timer—she's replacing Tommie, uh, Rebecca. Cindy—well—when she gets better, I'll use her on some better shows."

"Did any of them work with Crowell?"

"Julie and Cindy."

"Can I talk with them after the show?"

"I'll ask."

He finished his beer and waited; the three wafted away as rapidly as they arrived. Roberts and her friend seemed to be in no hurry.

"Are they all through now?"

"They're changing. They'll be here to pick up their checks. In this business, you don't write the checks until after a show. Too many part-timers fall through at the last minute."

"But you pay them promptly, Jeri," said the friend. "That's more than a lot of others do."

"Right. I pay them promptly."

Five minutes later, the blonde strode up. From the change of clothes and manner, Wager almost didn't recognize her. "Did it go all right?" she asked.

"Very good, Julie, dear, except you took too long between the second and third showings. Honey, twelve minutes is simply too long. You lose your audience."

"Don't blame me. Ann and I were ready—it was Cindy's hair."

"I understand, honey, and I'll ask her again to cut it." She signed a check. "Do you have time to talk to Detective Wager, here? He'd like to ask you some questions about poor Tommie."

The blonde studied him a long moment. "My daughter's waiting for me in the lobby. Can we talk there?"

"Sure."

"We'll have one more drink," said Roberts. "I'll ask Cindy to wait with us."

He followed the blonde into the hard glare of the lobby and away from the ears of the desk clerk, who stood wearily in the same spot. Wager saw that the model wasn't as young as she seemed in the dim light; the lines in her neck and beside her mouth said she was in her late twenties or early thirties. Still, she was one very good-looking woman, and those lines made her more interesting than a smooth, younger face. If Wager let himself, or had the time, he could wish she were half a foot shorter.

A ten-year-old girl with pale hair cropped like Mommy's sat perched on a plastic sofa guarding a scarred make-up kit. "This is my daughter." The girl stood and held out her hand like a small adult. Wager shook it, "Pleased to meet you, miss."

"Shall I wait over there, Mother?"

"We'll only be a few minutes, dear."

"Does your daughter come to all the shows?"

"Usually. For one thing, it saves baby-sitting money."

"And for another?"

Julie's smile was only half humorous. "She protects me from the customers."

"Do you need protection?"

He didn't mean that the way it sounded, and she had enough self-assurance not to be insulted. "Some of the men aren't interested in clothes."

"Does that happen often?"

"Often enough. You wanted to talk about Tommie. What did you want to ask?"

"Let's start with how well you knew her."

"Not very. We worked the same shows for several months. I didn't even know her real name."

"Did she ever meet any friends at these shows? Or leave with anyone she met?"

"Not that I know of. Jeri doesn't like that."

It was the same line of questions, the same reaching for more of Crowell's life, for the last names to the entries in her appointment book, for some link to the conservatory. The result was the same, too: Tommie Lee worked harder than most, had few if any friends, had only one thing on her mind—to be a top model. "I never saw her anywhere except at work; I try to spend as much time as I can with my daughter." Julie's glance went once more to the little girl, who sat drumming her heels against the plastic couch and watching Wager with eyes almost as distant and level as her mother's.

He didn't have to be told twice. "Thanks for your time, ma'am."

He returned to the dark lounge to make out Cindy seated close between Jeri Roberts and her friend. The two older women took turns speaking, and Cindy, clutching a pink glass filled with fruit slices and bushy leaves, nodded seriously.

"This is Detective Wager, Cindy, dear. He wants to ask you some questions about poor Tommie."

"Oh, that was so awful!"

"Can we go someplace else to talk? It's too noisy in here." And there were questions he wanted to ask without Roberts hearing.

"Well, Jeri's going to give me a ride home. I hate to keep her waiting."

"I'll give you a ride," said Wager.

"Well, I don't know.... What do you think, Jeri?"

Jeri Roberts looked hard at Wager and it crossed his mind that the woman might be a lesbian. A jealous one. "I'm sure Detective Wager will get you home safely. Here's your check, dear." She carved her name on the piece of paper.

"You're sure you don't mind?" Cindy asked.

"Of course not, dear."

"This is business." Wager smiled. "Strictly."

Or almost. He opened the door to the unmarked sedan. "I could use a cup of coffee. You want a drink or something?"

"I should get right home!"

Wager shrugged. "There are better places to talk than a police car."

She stood still. "This doesn't look much like a police car."

"There's the radio, miss." He leaned over and turned it on. "Handcuffs in the glove compartment, night stick on the door. I don't carry a shotgun." He keyed the microphone to show her he was real. "X-eighty-five. Give me a ten-thirty-six."

The correct time came back: "Twenty-thirty-two."

The girl finally managed a smile. "I've never been in a police car before."

Wager tried to remember some of the questions he'd been asked when, as a patrolman, he gave civilians a ride as part of the Citizen Awareness Program.

"This here's the channel selector." He flipped the switch. "It covers the four sectors of the City and County of Denver." He saw that the girl didn't give one small damn about frequencies, transmission ranges, codes, or security channels. But his talk put her at ease, and getting information was as much a matter of trade as of simply asking questions.

"You're sure you wouldn't like a cup of coffee?" he asked.

"Well, maybe not coffee. But something."

He pulled in to the parking lot of one of the half-dozen high-rise motels that faced across Quebec Street to the distant red dots that rode the towers and ramps of the air terminal. This lounge had more lights than the Jetliner but was furnished in the same smooth blankness designed for ease of cleaning. Except that here someone had cleaned.

Wager had coffee; Cindy ordered a margarita and tried to look old enough to know how to hold the glass. She had just turned nineteen, had been with Jeri for almost six months, just loved modeling more than anything else in the world, and loved working for Jeri because she learned so much.

"Were you a good friend of Rebecca's?"

"It sounds funny to hear Tommie called that. But she didn't really have what I'd call friends. I mean she was nice, and all. A lot of times after shows, Jeri buys us girls a drink to unwind with; sometimes it's just awful uptight, especially if there's a lot of buyers in the audience. Anyway, Tommie was real nice and had a good time and all, but . . ." Cindy's blue eyes rounded as she tried to come up with the right word.

"She didn't go out of her way to make friends?" suggested Wager.

"That's right! It was like she was just visiting and had her mind on where she was going instead of where she was."

"Did she get along with Jeri?"

"Oh, yes! A lot of people think Jeri's—well—hard. But she's not. Not when you really know her. She's real nice, and she's done a lot for me, and she did a lot for Tommie, even if..." The blue eyes widened again.

"If what?"

"Well, they didn't really have an argument; I mean, Jeri was angry, but it wasn't like they were fighting." She was unsure how much more to say.

Wager guessed. "This was when Tommie wanted to go to New York or San Francisco?"

"Oh, you already know about it!" A slight giggle. "I forget you're a detective—you really don't look like one. That's why I was kind of afraid to get in the car with you. I always thought detectives were—well, kind of taller."

"Tell me about Tommie and Jeri," said Wager.

"There's not much: a little while ago, Tommie asked for the names of some people to see in New York, and Jeri said she would be better off staying in Denver, but Tommie said she was going even if Jeri wouldn't give her some contacts."

"That made Jeri mad?"

"More, disgusted."

"What about Tommie?"

"What about her?"

"Was she mad, too?"

"No. I don't think Tommie ever got mad, not even when something went wrong at a show. She just got kind of thoughtful."

"Do things go wrong a lot?"

"Oh, let me tell you! And always when a number's ready to go out. Like tonight, my hair just wouldn't stay up; I guess I washed it too close to the show. Jeri was awful about it. She gets mad awful easy."

"Why don't you cut your hair?"

"I don't want to! Jeri says I should, but I don't want to."

It had only been a question, not a challenge. Wager got back to Crowell. "How long ago did she and Jeri have their argument?"

Cindy thought a moment. "Three weeks—at the time of The Denver's Christmas preview."

"Did you hear it?"

"No. Jeri told us about it after the show. She was upset because she didn't think Tommie was ready for New York."

"Do you want to go there?"

"You bet! That's the only place if you're a model, and Jeri says if I keep working as hard as I have been, maybe in a year or so I can go." She took a tiny sip at the salt-crusted rim of the glass. "She knows some real important people there who can get me started, but she doesn't want to waste their time by sending somebody who's not ready."

"Would Tommie have done all right there?"

"Well . . ." A person shouldn't talk unfriendly of the dead. "Jeri said she would have a hard time."

172

"But she was going anyway."

"I think around January. I remember she said her lease was up so she could go anytime." Another tiny sip. "I remember now, she was going home after Christmas shows and then go to New York from there. I forget where she said home was."

"She didn't talk much about home?"

"No, I guess we really didn't talk much about anything but modeling."

Wager refilled his cup from the small silver coffeepot warming over a candle. By now, the facts were familiar, but he was getting something else, something that couldn't be called fact but may have been more important. He groped for a way to move closer to the thing he was after. "Did you ever see Tommie date anybody from a show?"

"Jeri would be furious!"

"Even customers?"

"That's different—that's not really a date. It's just business."

"Did she ever go out with the same person a lot?"

"Oh, no. The sales staff only comes through town two or three times a year."

"Did you ever go out with her and one of these customers?"

"A few times, but I don't know that much about the business yet." She giggled slightly. "And sometimes I get asked for my I.D."

"You've never had any trouble with any of the men?"

"Only one." Cindy stared at the table and her shoulders hunched into a slight shudder.

"What happened?"

It took another sip. "He kept talking about how models knew more about their own bodies than any other women, and how this made them more sensuous. He said they liked to pose, and that every model he knew had to get relief from all the 'sensuous energy' they stored up." Another shudder. "Then he wanted me to go up to his room and see the pictures of the models he used in San Francisco."

"Did Tommie ever go out with this man?"

"No. I told Jeri what happened and she said it was the first and last time she'd accept any business from him. She's really sensitive about the agency's reputation."

"Do you like working at places like the Jetliner?"

Cindy studied the question. "I don't think anybody really likes it; it's dark and nobody can see the numbers. But Jeri's always there to make sure nothing happens, and she says it's good training. A model has to handle all sorts of situations, she says."

"So the truck drivers don't upset you?"

"They used to. I mean, some of the things they say show they think models are—well, not nice."

"But you don't mind now?"

"You get used to it. And Jeri says that most of them don't mean anything by it. Every now and then somebody gets obnoxious, but most of the men are shy— they don't really know what to say to a model." That small giggle. "Like you."

Wager had never called himself shy—he had nothing to be shy about; he just had good manners was all. He asked very politely, "Would you like another?"

"Oh, no. I shouldn't have had this one—it's all calories and salt. But I don't have another show for a week." She pushed at the damp foot of the glass. "I think Jeri was really angry about my hair. But I really don't want to cut it."

"Don't a lot of models have long hair?"

"Oh, gosh, yes! Farrah Fawcett's one. Of course she's got a lot of other things, too."

It sounded like an Arabic plumbing device, but Wager nodded and said, "There, you see?" Cindy was quickly happy again, and it seemed to him that this little girl would need a hell of a lot of luck in life. "Do you have a portfolio?"

"Yes. The school puts one together for us."

"Who's the photographer?"

"Les Tanaka was mine. He's real good; I think he does all the photography for the school."

"Have you ever heard of Phil Bennett or High Country Profiles?"

"I sure have! I heard I'd better stay away from him. Jeri doesn't like that man at all!"

"Why?"

"He rips-off people. He tells them they need a lot of expensive training before he can put together a portfolio."

"Did Tommie have any work done by him?"

"I wouldn't think so. But not just for the money. Jeri says that he tries to . . . to seduce every girl who goes there. Tommie just didn't seem to be the type who'd put up with that."

"You're sure Bennett acts that way?"

"Well, Jeri said so. And she knows just everybody in

the business."

Wager drove the girl home. On the way she told him that yes, her parents worried a little about her being a model; but no, once they knew a little more about the business and had met Jeri, they didn't mind the cost of the school. Especially now that she was starting to make some money, and her daddy even bragged a little to the neighbors.

He walked her to the door of the split-level home set on the bend of a curving street in one of the many suburban developments whose name ended in "wood." The porch light glowed and a man's shadow rested against the curtains of the picture window.

"Daddy's watching television." She hesitated on the top step, not quite sure how a woman of the world said good night to a detective. "Thank you for a lovely evening."

"And thank you for your help," said Wager.

13

Wager's first call after he got off work the next morning, Friday, was to the Famous Faces Modeling School. The moist, hot voice said it would be very happy to help with the two things he asked about: yes, the school's photographer was Les Tanaka. "His number is 794-5541! and our records don't list Tommie Lee as working for us at any time on the nineteenth, Detective Wager!"

"Thank you."

"You're welcome!"

He felt like swabbing his ear with a towel. The Tanaka number rang eight times before an entirely different voice answered, "Hello?"

"Is this Mr. Les Tanaka?" He wondered why so many Japanese-Americans gave their children names that began with L's or R's.

"It is," said the mild, deliberate voice.

"I'm Detective Wager investigating the death of Tommie Lee. Can I come over and talk with you?"

"Certainly. Do you know my address?"

Wager didn't; the mild voice gave him a number on West Alamo in distant Littleton. It took almost an hour to make the drive south through heavy traffic and strings of lights that turned red as he approached each one, and he hoped it wasn't going to be one of those days.

The building on the corner was a remodeled gas

station. Concrete aprons led from both streets, and in place of gas pumps, the service islands held large clay flowerpots filled with frost-killed petunias. The outside doors to the automobile bays were walled up with concrete block and whitewashed over, but except for removing the cash register and racks for oil cans, little had been done to the small office with its large windows and single concrete step. The room was empty. "Mr. Tanaka?"

"In here, please." The voice came through a door leading to the bays. Wager looked in to see the slight figure of a young man twisting the collar of a light stand. In the glare of some twenty bulbs and cushioned starkly against a sloping background of white cardboard sat a jar of green olives.

Wager showed his badge. "You're doing an advertising picture?"

"Yes. The client's Ollie the Olive. I think I'll call it 'Ollie's Story.'"

Wager could not tell if the shorter man's black eyes smiled or not. "Is this your usual type of job?"

"No—this one pays money." He screwed the surprisingly small camera onto its tripod and peered down into the square viewfinder. "Let me finish this series." Giving the aperture a gentle turn, he pressed the cable trigger, then cranked the film forward and peered again. Wager counted six pictures. "O.K., I think Ollie's happy now." He turned off the hot lights that had flooded the windowless room. "It's very difficult to make an olive say 'cheese.'"

"Is it easier with live models?"

"Rarely. As a matter of fact, I think I prefer the

178

olive."

"But you do the photography work for the Famous Faces Modeling School?"

"That's why I prefer the olive." He led Wager back into the office and gestured at a chair. "What may I help you with?"

Wager wasn't exactly sure. He had the same feeling last night when he was talking to Cindy: something was there, just out of sight, but he had no idea what it was or in what direction it lay. Still, a man couldn't catch fish without casting lines; he showed the picture to Tanaka. "Have you seen this woman before?"

Like Kramer, this photographer glanced at the back of the paper before studying the smiling girl. "Sure. It's Tommie Lee. I heard she had gone over to the enemy."

"Bennett?"

"Yes. He can't stand the Famous Faces School—and vice versa."

"Do you get along with him?"

"Oh, business could be better, but it's not worth fighting over. Besides, Phil's not a bad photographer. This isn't a bad shot. Well, not too bad."

"Does much of your work come from Famous Faces?"

"More work than money."

"Don't they pay their bills?"

"Sure—who couldn't pay what they offer? But for the work I do, it's not enough." He reached into a steel filing cabinet and pulled out two canisters of film. "Here's one girl's day—forty shots. That should take"—he shrugged—"two hours, maybe. With the sweet young things of Famous Faces, it's an all-day labor."

"Why don't you do something else?"

"Half a loaf, and all that; the girls pay fair prices, but I have to kick back 50 percent to Famous Faces. Still, I don't know what I'm complaining about. If I wasn't doing that, I probably wouldn't be doing anything. The world has only so many olives. Which Jeri, bless her heart, knows."

Wager glanced out a large window at the surrounding neighborhood, one that long ago changed halfway from single-family homes to the neighborhood's commercial block before the money ran somewhere else. "It's kind of a long way for the models to come, isn't it?"

"Low overhead. I underbid the competition. I even underbid myself. But when I get rich, friend, then you'll see a real studio."

"When did you do the pictures for Miss Crowell— Tommie Lee?"

He scooted his chair on squealing casters across the concrete to a small shelf of ledgers, "In"—his fingers ran up one page and down another—"April of this year. The twelfth through the fifteenth."

"It took a whole week?"

"Four days—Monday through Thursday."

"Do they all take that much time?"

"The school tuition pays for two days—the first is a dry run, then one day of real shooting. Black-and-white only. The third day's optional: some color work as well as more black-and-white, offered at reduced rates for students of Famous Faces only. Almost all of the girls want the option; Jeri talks them into it. For half." One dark eye winked at Wager. "And to tell you the truth, I don't hurry the girls through. I have more time than I do film."

"Why the extra day for Tommie Lee?"

"She didn't like the ones we did Tuesday and Wednesday. And I can't blame her. They were as lousy as anyone else's."

"Couldn't she pose in front of a camera?"

"Not as poorly as some, but not very well. Even she saw that. That was one thing about her."

"What was?"

"She did have a good eye—even for herself, which is one of the hardest things for a would-be model to learn. Most of the people when they see themselves think the picture's great. It can be god-awful, but if they recognize their own face, it's great art. If people weren't like that, Famous Faces would be out of business. And I'd be a tax burden."

"So you gave her an extra day's work?"

"Gave? She paid for it, friend. Cash." He put the ledger back. "But don't tell that to Jeri, will you? If one of the girls wants extra shots, I knock off 10 percent and tell her to keep quiet about it—what Jeri doesn't know about, she doesn't collect on. But if she ever does find out, there'll be no more *gohan* for old Tanaka-san."

"*Gohan?*"

"Japanese for 'rice.'"

"Why did Tommie Lee switch over to Bennett?"

"I told her to. Well, I told her to try another photog. She didn't like any of the shots, and she wouldn't believe that it wasn't the camera. It's my business to make cameras lie, but I can only do so much."

"Do you tell a lot of the students to try someone else?"

"Hell, no! Fortunately, I don't have to; most of them are happy with what they see because they see pretty pictures of themselves."

"But you told Miss Lee?"

"Some models do come out better for different photogs, and Tommie was very serious about this modeling crap. More so than most of the ones I've seen. So I suggested that perhaps she could do better work for another person."

"And you mentioned Bennett?"

"Among others. I don't know why she picked him. Perhaps because he's at the head of the alphabet. I wonder if I should change my name to Akido?"

"Did she do any better for him?"

"There's your answer." He pointed to the photograph Wager held. "She's pretty, she's smiling, she's boring. A model's got to do better than that. The best really come alive in a picture."

"The photographer can't do that for them?"

"Perhaps—if they have the time and patience. But I don't think there's a photographer in Denver who's that good, including me. No, it saves a lot of time and expense if the model's got it to start with. Then anyone can work with her. That's why the top models make so much."

Wager remembered someone else talking about the special vitality that was missing from Crowell's pictures: Pitkin. Who, in his own way, was something of a photographer. "Did she ever tell you about any of her friends or acquaintances?"

"No. Models aren't paid to talk. Not in front of a still camera, anyway, and except for the video-tape rushes that I don't handle, Famous Faces didn't offer much training in motion work." He paused. "Perhaps that's why she went to Bennett—he does audio stuff as well as still and motion photography. If she was interested in voice-overs and motion, Bennett would have all the equipment in one studio."

"Did you ever see her after she went to him?"

"No."

"Did you talk to him about her?"

"I try not to talk to him about anything. Frankly, I don't like the guy."

"Why?"

Tanaka smiled. "He refers to me as 'the inscrutable unscrupulous.'"

"What do you call him?"

"Ah, that's very good—and you're right: I've responded to an epithet with an epithet. In my mind, he's 'the aperture man.'"

"Aperture man?"

"He's always trying to adjust his models' apertures."

"Doesn't messing around like that hurt business?"

Tanaka looked puzzled. "What does that have to do with business unless someone gets raped? This is the exciting world of low fashion, and a lot of the girls like to feel excited. They think it's the fashion. And Bennett's one of those low ones who develops more than film in his darkroom."

"Did he have something going with Tommie Lee?"

"I don't know, but it's possible. I hear that every woman he meets receives a standing offer."

"Do you know any of Bennett's friends?"

"He has mistresses and ex-mistresses. I've never met anyone who was his friend."

"Why?"

"In this racket everyone uses everyone else, but Bennett's a little worse than most. He uses people in a way that leaves them feeling . . . insulted."

"Can you give me the name of an ex-mistress?"

"Perhaps." Tanaka squeaked back across the floor and thumbed the pages of one of the ledgers. "You might talk with Ginger Eaton—I hope that's a professional name—her number's 761-0574."

"Can I use your phone?"

"Why not? No one else wants to."

Ginger Eaton was waiting when he pressed the doorbell at the condominium on South Washington Avenue. "I saw you drive up." She reminded Wager of Julie—she had the same easy movement when she walked, the same self-assurance in her gaze. And though she was a little shorter and heavier than the blond woman, Miss Eaton seemed a few years younger. "I never met Tommie—I only read about it in the paper yesterday, so I don't know what I can tell you."

"I was more interested in hearing about High Country Profiles."

"Oh? Why?"

"She had some pictures made there before she was

killed. I'm trying to find out all I can about everything she did. Maybe something will turn up somewhere."

Miss Eaton led him to an overstuffed couch and sat on one end of it. "Well, ask away."

He sat at the other end. "I understand you had some work done there?"

"Yes. I certainly did."

"Was that with Mr. Bennett?"

"Yes to that, too."

"Is he a good photographer?"

The voice had a more decided tone this time: "One of the best in town."

"Has he been real successful in training models for better jobs?"

The woman tugged a cigarette from a round canister made to look like a small Coor's beer can and tapped it on the coffee table. "Who gave you my name?"

"Les Tanaka."

She lit it and looked at Wager through the thin smoke. "Why?"

"He said you had been friendly with Bennett."

"I see. Good old Les; he tries so hard to be casual." There was no ash yet on the tobacco, but she dragged it across the small ashtray. "Phil and I screwed, Detective Wager, but we weren't friends. Not for very long, anyway."

"I'd like to hear more about it."

"Again: why?"

"He may have been screwing Tommie Lee. It might tell me something about her."

"I'm sure he was—or at least tried to." Another

185

deep pull on the cigarette. "Do you think it might tell you whether or not she was a whore? She was a model, so she might as well be a whore, is that it?"

"No. But it might tell me who killed her."

"Do you mean Phil?"

"I don't mean anybody right now. I'm just trying to learn what I can about Rebecca Crowell and everybody she knew."

"Crowell—that was her real name, wasn't it?"

"Yes."

"Mmm." Another drag and she stubbed out the long butt. "All right. I'll be a good citizen—Phil Bennett is a son of a bitch. If that's what Les wanted you to hear, he sent you to the right person."

"Why should Les want that?"

"Because he was losing business—and other things—to Phil."

"A lot?"

"From what Phil told me, he was taking away about half of Les's customers."

"When was this?"

"A year ago. A year last week."

"That's when you went to Bennett? Were you with Tanaka before that?"

"Yes."

He wasn't quite sure how to get to the next point, and Miss Eaton offered no help; she sat on the couch with one leg folded beneath her and waited with the kind of blank expression that, Wager thought, gynecologists must recognize. "Did Bennett help you with your work?"

"Yes. I'll have to say he did. He is a good photographer."

"What makes him so good?"

She gazed across the compact living room with the serving counter between it and the kitchen, the sloping ceiling of the stairway, the tiny electric fireplace set down in what Wager thought was called a "conversation pit" but which looked more like a shallow foxhole. "I guess it was the way he could bring things out of you. Most of the time, you're over here, the camera's over there, and it's a real struggle to force yourself into that lens. With Phil, you know the camera's there . . . but he makes it *welcome* you. I guess that's not too clear. I'm sorry."

"What's he do that's different from, say, Tanaka?"

"Les's sessions are more . . . poised, cool. He makes you feel like one of those very still Chinese statues, and then he does a lot with the lights. Phil is just the opposite. He moves, he talks, he sings to you. You just feel . . . high. You feel like you're unfolding, opening up." The intensity faded from her voice. "It's a little like falling in love," she said flatly.

"Is that how it happened?"

"It?" Her lips twisted and she reached for another cigarette. "Yes, Detective Wager, 'it' happened that way."

"What went wrong?" He held the lighter for her.

"I unfolded. He pretended to. I suppose you could say he was like his own little camera—take, take, take. Except that when he was through, he laughed."

"Laughed?"

"It was as if all along he had been playing a trick— trying to see how much he could make a woman—

187

me—care for him. How many things she would do for him." Her mouth smiled prettily. "Would you like to hear the particulars?"

"No."

She looked away again. "Anyway, he has his methods of degrading a woman. Emotionally, I mean. It's as if he wants to see how far he can stretch those emotions before they break, as if he wants to make you know he can do anything with you. And he never stopped twisting and pulling."

"Has he done this to a lot of people?"

"As far as I'm concerned, one too many." Again the long butt was snuffed out. "If he did it to this Tommie Lee, I feel sorry for her."

"Did Les Tanaka have anything going with Tommie Lee before she went to Bennett?"

"I don't think so. If he did, it couldn't have been much."

"Why?"

She shrugged. "He still likes me. Good old Les."

Wager closed his notebook and stood. "Thanks for your help, Miss Eaton. I'm sorry I had to ask some of those questions."

Her voice was only half-mocking: "An old fashioned gentleman!"

"My Hispano heritage," he said, and paused at the door. "Did Bennett's portfolio work help you get better jobs?"

"Not exactly. But I manage to make ends meet." She leaned against the half-closed door. "I still do some modeling, Detective Wager." And that was all she would say.

14

This time it was the snap of the clock radio's timer that woke him. The green figures said 10:00—he had slept for ten hours, and to judge from the stiffness in his neck, most of that time had been without moving. And he was hungry. Turning on the television to let the scratchy voices of Friday night's John Wayne movie echo off the room's walls, he set a chicken breast under the oven grill and began boiling rice. Half a red onion for a little *fuerza*, a bit of garlic *para la corazón*, and a dish of those round peppers that look so cool and green but explode like cannon balls between the teeth. It was a bigger meal than he had eaten in days, and more sleep, too; so that when he called in to the division headquarters, he sounded almost happy.

"Great God—it's the Man of the Hour. Superdick himself." Ross's voice was loud over the background noise of a country-and-Western station.

"The one and only."

"Did you write that story yourself?"

"What story?"

"What story! The one in the *Post* tonight. By your good friend Gargan."

Wager didn't feel quite as happy. "I haven't seen it."

"I reckon your press agent has a few copies."

"Is there anything for me on the board?"

"Well, let's see. . . . There's a movie contract, and

189

the F.B.I. telegraphed to say they need some help with a tough case. . . ."

"Is there a report on an interview, Ross?"

"Underneath all these TV offers, yeah."

"Would you be kind enough to read it, please?" The Spanish inflection was back.

"How can I say no to such a renowned officer of the law, Detective Wager?" In the pause, he heard the crackle of a sheet of paper. "To: Denver's Most Famous Detective; From: Detective Hall, Peon Third Class; Subject: Interview with one George Brock, 1308 Garfield, Apartment 1." Ross waited for Wager's squawk.

He kept his mouth shut.

Ross continued, "Said Detective Hall interviewed said witness at his home at said address at 2:45 P.M., 29 October 1976. Said Witness stated that yes, Mr. Nick Mauro had been at home on Tuesday, 19 October. Witness remembers because he and Mr. Mauro did some work on the yard that morning. Mulching roses. Witness thinks Mr. Mauro ate lunch at home, but is not certain because he took his wife shopping just before noon, and when he came back, he did not see Mr. Mauro. The next time the witness saw Mr. Mauro that day was around four in the afternoon when Mr. Mauro came home from somewhere."

"Does he say whether Mauro owns a car?"

"No. And he doesn't say whether Mauro came home walking or driving. My, my—I'd better have a word with young Detective Hall; that kind of work is not up to your high demands."

"That's the whole report?"

"Filed sixteen-forty-five hours, Friday, 29 October."

"Thanks."

"Any time, Officer Wager. The detective bureau is eager to assist you in any way we can." Ross sounded happy that Wager sounded mad.

He had planned one stop on the way to work, but now added another: the local supermarket newsstand. Under a four-column picture of Rebecca Crowell bending backward in a draperylike evening dress, the story was headlined "SOUGHT FAME, FOUND DEATH." It began, "She had just turned 23 and came to the City with one overriding ambition: to be a model." Gargan's article ran on from there, quoting Mr. Crowell's puzzlement during a telephone interview that anyone would want to kill his daughter, and describing this reporter's shock to discover that no one had told the bereaved parents about the mutilation of their daughter's body. A smaller photograph showed the rounded shape of the conservatory; next to it was a shot of an abandoned car. The part of Gargan's feature story that pissed Ross off—and that would bring the bulldog down on Wager's neck again—came in the second long column of print: "Detective Gabriel Wager, who brings to the Homicide Division an outstanding reputation won in the Organized Crime Division of the District Attorney's office . . ." Gargan kept referring to him as the "renowned" or the "widely acclaimed" or the "greatly respected" police officer in charge of the investigation who had "promised an early solution to the crime." Readers were also told that this reporter was fortu-

191

nate enough to lend some assistance in locating Miss Crowell's former employers, the New Faces Modeling Agency. "Ms. Jeri Roberts, owner and manager of the agency, expressed shock and telephoned the girl's parents to express her sympathy." An earlier employer, Mr. William Pitkin of the Rocky Mountain Tax & Title Service, also expressed shock and said he remembered Miss Crowell as an attractive and hardworking employee who could have been whatever she wanted to be.

Folding the paper neatly into a compact pad, he slid it into a trash bin and headed for Elton's Place. Right now he had more to worry about than what the bulldog might make of Gargan's story.

The tavern was located eight blocks from Mauro's rooms in the middle of a series of single-story shops—cleaners, drugstore, shoe shop, hobby crafts. Its front window was painted blue with a hole left for a neon Budweiser sign. The door opened onto one end of the bar along which a Friday-night crowd of six customers sat staring at the television set over the far end. In the picture, a uniformed cop was busily thumping his riot stick on a black man's skull; Wager waited until an ad for men's cologne danced on, then caught the eye of the woman behind the bar.

"Hi—didn't see you come in." She smiled professionally.

That was because she sat beneath the television set like a cat watching a goldfish bowl. "Do you know Dominick Mauro?"

"Nick? Sure—he's right over there." The flabby arm pointed to a figure dim in the glow of a cigarette machine and settled comfortably at one of the few tables.

"Can you tell me if he was in here on the nineteenth? That's two Tuesdays ago."

The woman peered at Wager; her frizzy hair was bleached yellow like thick smoke and jiggled when she jerked her head. "Maybe you better ask Nick himself."

Wager showed his badge. "I'm asking you."

"Oh. Listen, this here's a family place, you know? We got our neighbors come in here. There ain't been no kind of trouble and we don't want none."

Wager smiled. "Then answer the question."

"You'll have to ask George. He's my husband. He worked all that week."

"All right. Where's George?"

"Goose-hunting. He left yesterday and won't be back until Sunday night."

"Where'd he go?"

"Nebraska. Up near Scotts Bluff. We got relatives got a ranch near there."

Two or three faces had turned down the bar to see what was keeping the woman from filling beer glasses.

"How about a draw," said Wager.

She pulled it and almost dropped the wet glass as she set it on the bar. "That's fifty cents."

Wager had the coin ready. "Thanks."

She turned back to the television picture where now the black man wore bandages and shouted angrily at a white police chief. Wager went to Mauro's table and sat without a word.

The thick-bodied man squinted at him. "What the hell you doing here?"

"Asking about your activities on Tuesday, October 19th."

"The hell you are!"

"You spent part of the morning helping your landlord fix his roses. Around noon you left. You came back home about four. Where'd you go?"

Mauro's mouth hung slightly open. "I'll be goddamned. You really have been poking your goddamned nose into my life, ain't you?"

"Where'd you go that day?"

"Maybe I don't want to tell you!"

"That's your privilege." Wager smiled for the second time in five minutes; he was beginning to feel like Mr. Sunshine. "If you're sure you want it that way."

Caution came into Mauro's voice. "What do you mean by that?"

"I mean if I don't find out from you, I start asking all your friends. I tell everybody you know that I'm a cop and that I'm interested in your whereabouts on the day that a murder was committed."

"Murder? You think I had something—? I didn't even know that cunt!"

Most people would have said they'd never seen her or never met her. "Your friends will believe that, won't they?" He aimed a thumb at the bar.

Mauro glanced at the woman bartender. When she saw his eyes, her face jerked back to the television set. "You sons of bitches ain't changed in twenty years." he said.

"But you have. You've paid your debt to society;

now you're an honest citizen. What's an honest citizen like you got to hide?"

"You ain't getting me on no murder!"

"Somebody put that head in the conservatory, Mauro. Somebody with a key."

Even in the dim light, Wager saw the worry gather in wrinkles around the man's eyes. "It wasn't me, goddamn you! There's lots of keys to that place!"

"No. There's not. There's six. I know the whereabouts of five. You are number six."

Mauro licked at his lower lip and then drained the beer glass. "I . . . I went—let's see, I went to the grocery store. And then took the groceries home. And then—Christ, I can't remember! That was almost two weeks ago. What the fuck were you doing two weeks ago?"

"Where'd you go after the grocery store?"

"Let's see. . . . Cheesman Park! I drove over to the park and walked around a while—fed the ducks."

"Did you meet anybody?"

Mauro looked up. "You mean did I meet somebody who'd remember I was there?"

"Yes."

"I bought some peanuts from that guy with the push wagon—you know the one. He might remember. Maybe."

"Then where'd you go?"

"I drove back home. Then I came over here for a beer."

"What time was that?"

"I don't know! Midafternoon. Ask George—we talked about goose-hunting. He was going goose-hunting and we talked about that."

"What time did you leave here?"

"I guess four. Maybe five."

"What'd you do that night?"

"I don't know.... I watched TV, I guess. I can't remember if I came back here or not."

"Did you go anywhere else?"

"No. I'd remember that. I don't remember doing nothing special, so I must of just watched TV or come here."

"What kind of car do you have?"

"A Chevy Impala—'72."

Wager caught the woman peeking their way again and signaled for two beers. She drew them and seemed relieved that he and Mauro were now good drinking buddies. "Who's the Elton the place is named after?" Wager asked her.

"Ain't nobody, really." Her heavy lips lifted in another professional smile. "I'm Mary and my husband's George, and our last name's Smith. We wanted something with a little more class than that, but still had a neighborly sound."

"You picked a good name."

The lips smiled thanks, and she went back to the cash register and the television.

Wager drank in silence; Mauro stared down at the strings of bubbles rising in his beer. "You're sure you never saw the dead woman before?" Wager asked.

"Yes, I'm sure!" But the worry still hung around the man like a bad smell.

15

When Wager reported for duty at midnight on Sunday, the twenty-four-hour board held a lab report of the complete inventory of Crowell's apartment, a note from the motor vehicles section saying the Crowell car had been found, and a clipping of Gargan's article with Wager's name and the adjectives circled in red pencil by Ross. Wager dropped that into the trash can. There was also a short note from Doyle, and he saved that for last.

The Mustang had been found locked and apparently abandoned in the 3600 block of Irving Street in northwest Denver. It had been ticketed once for obstructing the street cleaner's weekly tour down that side of the pavement; after the second ticket, it was towed to the police garage and impounded. Somehow the officer writing the tickets did not know—or care—that the vehicle was being sought; it turned up during a routine inventory of the police compound. Wager knew the area where the car was left, a mixture of small houses and older apartments; there weren't enough garages, and many residents parked on the streets. No one would notice one more car. Searching over the city-county map with its color-coded pins showing clusters of various crimes, he found Irving Street, and yes, three streets away a major bus line ran downtown. Crowell could have left the car there herself; that was a possibility and he would take her photograph through the neighborhood to see if anyone recognized the girl. But he didn't think they would. His guess was that the killer drove her car to a place where he could leave it without attracting attention, then caught a bus downtown—a taxi would be too easy to trace through the dispatcher's records. He also guessed that the car wouldn't tell them a thing, but he dialed the lab number anyway. Baird answered.

"This is Gabe Wager, Fred. I'd like you to go over a vehicle down in the compound. A 1970 Ford Mustang, Colorado AR-3753."

Baird repeated the description and number. "Can it wait until tomorrow? That place is darker than hell at night; I wouldn't be able to see much."

"Sure; I don't think you'll find anything, anyway. It's Rebecca Crowell's car."

"Right—I got a good set of her prints here. We'll see if anything else shows."

Wager pulled her file from the drawer marked "ACTIVE: CURRENT CASES UNSOLVED" and read the pathologist's report one more time. Then he called Baird back again.

"Did the F.B.I. ever send an answer on the fibers found in the wound?"

"Wait one."

He waited.

"Gabe? It came in two or three days ago, and somebody filed it without forwarding a copy to you. Sorry."

"What's it say?"

"The tests run were spectroscopy, microcrystallization, chromatography, and neutron activation analysis."

"What did they come up with, Fred?"

"Not a hell of a lot. The fiber samples were too small to do much with, so most of the report's inconclusive. But it's a nylon of thin diameter, probably the kind used for underwear, nightgowns, that kind of thing. There's another fiber trace, cotton. That corroborates the hypothesis, it says here, because many manufacturers use a blend of nylon and cotton for nightgowns, and there was no spandex, which is used in undergarments. The samples weren't big enough to get a composition, so there's no way to match them to any other cloth that turns up. That's about the best they can do for us."

"She was wearing a nightgown when she was killed?"

"Only probable; it's safer to guess she wore only one layer of clothes in that area. But I can't think of anything else it could have been. You can't go into court with that, though."

What the hell was she doing wearing a nightgown at the time of day when she was stabbed? "O.K.—read it again and let me get it down." He jotted the basic facts in his notebook and told Baird to send him an official copy of the report, then sat staring at the papers spread across his desk. Nightgown. Wager went to the inventory of the girl's belongings and marked off each item as he read the three-column list. Nothing seemed out of the ordinary; but tugging at the edge of his mind were the things missing from the list: not one picture by Tanaka, no other photographs except those found in the portfolio, no tapes or film rushes from High Country—maybe she kept only those pictures which could help her, and tossed the rest away; from what he knew, and liked about her, she didn't treat herself with much sentimentality. Nor did the list mention nightgowns. Underpants, brassières, a robe, but not one nightgown or even a pair of pajamas. He gathered the papers back into related piles and clipped them together, replacing the now thick folder in the file drawer. She had driven somewhere, had a little booze, put on a nightgown, and then got stabbed. But, goddamn it, no evidence of sex. And whoever killed her tossed her body away like garbage but treated her head like an idol. It was not as crazy as it seemed. Weird, yes; but insane, no, because there was some kind of motive and there was a fear of consequences. Wager slammed the drawer shut and thought of the worried look in Mauro's eyes.

The last item from the twenty-four-hour board was the note from Doyle: "See me in the morning before you leave." He had a good idea what that was about. Slipping his radio pack into his jacket pocket, he dropped that note into the trash can, too. Before he saw the bulldog or anybody else, he had his eight hours of duty to put in.

Doyle was waiting when he ended his tour Monday morning. "You got a minute, Wager?"

It wasn't a question. He followed the chief into the cubicle crammed with files, duty charts, statistics, pamphlets, and reviews, and its own white plastic coffee maker.

"I read that *Post* article on the Crowell case," said Doyle.

"Yes, sir."

"The reporter—what's his name? Gargan?—seemed to know a lot about it."

"He asked me some questions, but most of it he found out on his own."

"He also found out you're Jesus Christ come back, didn't he?"

"I didn't see his story before he filed," said Wager. "And I didn't do him any special favors. I answered what questions I could just like the procedure manual says to."

Doyle poured himself a cup of coffee. "I also read something else—Meyer's report. He said you were bent out of shape that I asked him to talk to you."

He could imagine how the S.I.B. man wrote it up, and he could have made an excuse. But he didn't. "Yes, sir."

"Why?"

Wager wondered if that was a serious question. "Putting the S.I.B. on me? That doesn't show much confidence, does it, Captain?"

"Confidence isn't something I give. It's got to be earned."

Which was something that went both ways. "My work's good in every division I've been in."

"But you've never been in *my* division before. And this is your first homicide case. And it's one which is not routine. And, by God, when I delegate authority to someone—S.I.B. or otherwise—it's *my* authority they've got." He paused, but Wager said nothing; there was no sense wasting words. "Did you talk to this reporter before or after you talked to Meyer?"

"Both. Gargan's been on the story since the beginning, and I saw him Thursday afternoon at the Botanic Gardens." What the hell was Doyle after now? "Why?"

"Here's why. On one day, Meyer tells you to let the case wait for your partner to get back. On the next day, this reporter's telling the world that you're the best thing since Sherlock Holmes and that you've got the case sewed up. The thought did cross my mind, Wager, that maybe you used this reporter to make sure you kept the case."

It took a minute for that to sink in, and when his words came, they had a very strong Spanish inflection. "Meyer, he told me you wanted to know how the case was going—that you wanted to be sure it wasn't a waste of time and interfering with my other duties. In my judgment, Captain, and as the officer of record, the case is going all right. Not good, but all right. As for that crap in the newspapers, Captain, I don't play those games."

The bulldog looked at him for a long moment. "I'm glad to hear it. Because that kind of glory-hunting tears a division apart. And I won't stand for it. I want a team, not a collection of self-seeking individuals."

Wager didn't give a damn for teams, but he knew what Doyle meant. And he generally agreed with the chief. Cops had to work together—there were too few of them not to. But a man also felt pride in doing a little better than anybody else wearing the same label. "Yes, sir."

Doyle motioned to the coffee maker on its stand with the several cups upside down beside it. "You

202

want some coffee? I want you to fill me in on where the case is now."

It was a cautious peace offer. Wager accepted just as cautiously: "Black."

He left the bulldog's office some forty-five minutes later with Doyle's last sentence in his ears: "The case is still yours, Wager. But don't take chances with any part of it. Your partner reports back in four days, and you'll have some help then."

Wager stopped off at his desk to make one call; Lisa Dahl answered, "Rocky Mountain Tax & Title Service."

"This is Detective Wager. Can I talk to William Pitkin?"

"Yes." It wasn't an old friend's voice. "Just a moment."

"This is Bill Pitkin."

"Can you tell me what kind of nightgown or pajamas Rebecca Crowell used?" It was something that still bothered him.

"I never saw her wear any—and not just because . . . well, you know."

"Did she sleep naked?"

"I do recall her saying that she didn't like to wear anything to bed because she rolled and tossed and got twisted up. We—ah—sort of joked about it."

"Thanks."

Pitkin didn't hang up. "You didn't tell me that she was the one who had been decapitated."

"That's right. I didn't tell you."

"The reporter said the funeral would be in Kansas City. Is that right?"

"I think so."

"I see. Well, that's really too far to go. But don't you think that the office should send flowers?"

The office should send. "That's up to you, Pitkin. You and Lisa Dahl."

The man's silence was brief. "I suppose it is, Good-bye."

Wager drove to the Botanic Gardens and parked in the employee lot. The gabby groundskeeper with the bifocals was the only person in Greenhouse 1.

"Is Nick Mauro around?"

"You're the policeman! How's things going on that murder case?"

"I'm still working on it, Mr. Duncan. Is Mauro around?"

"That was a terrible thing. I read that story in the paper. I don't know that the reporter should of put in a picture of the conservatory, though; Mr. Sumner sure didn't like that. But that poor girl. I feel real sorry for her parents. They seem like such nice folks."

"Yes, sir. Is—?"

"Nick? No. It's a bit early yet. He should be here soon if you want to wait, though."

Wager should have remembered; maybe he was getting old—or tired—or maybe there was no difference. "No, thanks. Will you tell him that I was asking for him?"

"If that's what you want, I sure will."

Mauro's apartment was empty, or at least no one answered his knock; Wager tore a blank page from his little book and slipped a note under the door: "Gabe Wager dropped by." He thought of going past

Elton's Place but decided against it. For now, it was enough just to leave messages; besides, he was too goddamned tired.

His shower over, Wager was dressing for the next tour of duty when the telephone rang. Gargan's voice asked if he had seen Friday's story on the Crowell murder.

"I did."

"Ross says you didn't like it much."

Wager almost told him exactly how much, but Gargan's voice was poised to laugh. "The first time I read it, I thought you laid it on kind of thick. But when I read it again, it didn't seem too bad, Gargan."

"What?"

"I said I liked the story. Maybe I'll make Senior Detective because of it."

"You're shitting me, Wager!"

"No—I'm serious. I liked it. It's nice to be appreciated, for a change. I tell you what—I go on duty in an hour and a half. Meet me at the Frontier and I'll buy you a drink."

"I don't think so—I got a story to file."

"*And* I'll tell you something about the Crowell case."

"Like what?"

"I'll see you there." Wager hung up and tugged his jacket on; before he could get out the door, the telephone rang again. It was still jangling when he left.

He just beat the wrestling fans to his favorite booth near the Frontier's serving window. They pushed in noisily from the Convention Center Arena across the street, trying to keep their sweaty and screaming world with them a little longer. Excited faces turned this way and that to shout at other faces, and beefy women still giggled at the craziness of The Crusher or Gonzo the Gorilla as they towed baggy-eyed kids who wriggled with nervous energy and late-hour whines. Through the calls for beer and the howling "did-you-see"s Gargan pushed and tugged his way to the booth.

"Jesus, you pick such nice places!"

"I like it." He signaled Rosie, who stopped by on her way to the wrestling fans. "Martini?" Gargan nodded. Wager ordered a beer for himself and told Rosie to make the martini a double.

"We can't talk in this place, Wager!"

"They'll quiet down soon. Here's to your story—thanks a lot."

Gargan's eyes narrowed slightly as he sipped his drink. "Sure, Gabe. Ross was really wrong in telling me you didn't like fulsome praise, right?"

"I don't know what 'fulsome' means. But I sure like praise." He waved to Rosie for another round.

"Jesus—I just started this one!"

"She's busy. By the time they get here, we'll be ready."

Gargan's shoulders bobbed. "You're buying."

Wager lifted his beer glass and smiled.

"You said you had something more on the Crowell case."

"Right. But it's really sensitive stuff. I wouldn't tell you except you did something for me. Now I want to do something for you."

"Sensitive like what?"

"You sound suspicious, Gargan. I'm trying to thank you for what you did and you act like I'm a sack full of snakes."

"It doesn't seem like the real you, Gabe."

"What's not? Gratitude? Tell me the last time you did something I could be grateful for."

"True, but—"

"And when a debt's owed, it's got to be paid. That's part of my colorful Hispano heritage."

Gargan popped the olive from his martini into his mouth and stared at Wager through the dim light. Then he reached to grasp Wager's shoulder. "Aw, you don't owe me anything, Gabe!" He gulped a mouthful of his drink. "In fact . . . you really want to know something funny?"

"I sure do."

"When I wrote that story"—he glanced up and grinned—"I wanted to piss you off."

"Is that a fact!"

"Don't get me wrong, Gabe—you're a good cop. A lot of people—other cops included—don't like you. But you're a good cop." Gargan scratched at his head. "Maybe not much of a human being, but a god-damned good cop. I really got to tell you that."

"It's nice of you to say that, Gargan."

"Well, the thing's this: when I wrote the story, I tried to make you look like you told me what to write—that you wanted all the credit for everything. I mean, I tried like hell to make it look like there wasn't anybody else on that case but you and God, and that you were in charge."

"I'll be damned! The joke's on me." Gargan's glass

was almost empty. Wager looked around for Rosie, to order another round.

"No, man—that's just the point. Here you take it seriously, and the whole goddam thing's turned around. Now the joke's on me."

"Ain't that something," said Wager.

"No hard feelings for what I was trying to do? Really?"

"Would I hurt my press agent?"

Gargan's thin mustache bobbed from side to side and finally settled in decision, "Gabe—whatever I might have thought about you is forgotten. You are 100 percent!"

They touched glasses and drank. Wager ordered another round.

"You ever heard of Klipstein? Gerald Klipstein?" he asked the reporter.

"Who hasn't? He's got more deals than a deck of outhouse cards."

"As well as being a civic leader."

"The civicest. What about him?"

"He's tied to the Crowell murder."

"How the hell's anybody like Klipstein tied to Crowell?"

"Shhh. That's why the thing's so sensitive."

"Clue me in, Wager!"

"Guess who the chairman of the board for the Botanic Gardens is?"

"No shit?"

Wager glanced around the room that was slowly emptying of the wrestling fans, then pulled out a brochure that described the gardens and its worthy aims. "Look." His fingernail tapped the list of board members.

"Son of a bitch! But—"

"I'm coming to that. Tell me, how was access gained to the conservatory?"

"The lab report said someone used a key." Gargan's eyes widened and blinked. "Him?"

"There's only six keys. The chairman of the board has one. And . . ." Wager frowned and shook his head. "No. I can't tell you that yet. But we have reason to believe he knows a hell of a lot more than he's told us." He leaned a little closer. "And we'll find out tonight."

"When tonight. What are you after?"

Wager beckoned toward the pale circle of face with its smudge of mustache in the middle. "We leaked just enough information to worry him. Now we think he'll try a run for Nicaragua tonight."

"Nicaragua?" The reporter's eyes blinked again. "They don't have an extradition treaty!"

"That's it."

"How do you know it's tonight?"

"We're not positive, but an informant tells us he bought a ticket on a flight leaving at 12:20 A.M. for Chicago. Now, there just happens to be a nonscheduled flight leaving Chicago for Mexico City at six-thirty tomorrow morning. We're waiting to hear from the Chicago police whether or not he's got a ticket on that flight. If he does, we're going to be waiting right here at the airport to say, 'Mr. Klipstein, we'd like to ask you a few questions.'"

"Holy shit—Klipstein! He's really big. And taking off for Nicaragua! It sounds like a goddam TV drama."

"Don't it, though."

Gargan looked at his watch. "His flight leaves at twelve-twenty? Man, it's almost midnight now! This could be the story of the year—let's go!"

"Jesus, I didn't know it was so late." Wager called Rosie over and paid. He followed Gargan's rapid lurch into the cold and empty streets that were downtown Denver after eleven at night. "Hold on a minute, Gargan—I've got to stop by headquarters to see if they've heard from Chicago. You start for the airport. If the move's on, we'll come up behind you running hot—lights and siren. Then you haul ass to the airport."

"Right!" The reporter sprinted for the plain brown Ford with the press tag and swerved it, wheels shrieking, around the corner.

Wager pulled the antenna out of his radio pack: "This is X-eighty-five."

"Go ahead," said the dispatcher's level voice.

"I have a tip on a suspect driving a brown Ford sedan with Colorado press plates, number 185. Suspect is said to be drunk and possibly repeat possibly armed and dangerous. Last seen driving at high speed north on Fifteenth Street, probably headed for Stapleton International."

"Ten-four."

210

16

Wager knew little would come of showing Crowell's picture around Irving Street, but it had to be done. Besides, it was still too early in the morning to visit Mauro; he'd learned that yesterday. Parking near where the Crowell vehicle had been ticketed, he began knocking on doors. It took an hour; no one in any of the small homes or sagging row houses had ever seen the girl. That corroborated what Baird told him last night—that the steering wheel and the various handles and mirrors of her car had been wiped clean by someone, and that the only prints found on the trunk or in the back seat belonged to the victim.

He said "Thank you" at the final door and checked his watch. With time out for breakfast—or supper— he should reach the Botanic Gardens when Mauro was just starting work.

The heavyset man was walking slowly with a bag and trash-pick down the side of a walk when Wager arrived. He let Mauro, face to the ground, come close enough to be startled when he saw Wager's legs planted in front of him.

"Goddamned!"

"Don't be nervous, Nick. I just stopped by to say hello."

The rusted iron needle leaped at a paper cup. "Why didn't you just leave another goddam note?"

"Because you have something to tell me."

"What's that?"

"I don't know. But you do."

"I got nothing to say to you! I say to you leave me the hell alone!"

"Tell me what it is, and I'll leave you alone. It's going to happen sooner or later; do it now and save us both all this crap."

The man's barrel chest rose and fell and he twisted his head back and forth on its thick neck to glare along the path leading through tangles of bare rose branches. Wager watched the tip of the trash-pick twitch upward once, twice. He didn't think Mauro would do it—but the graveyards were full of cops who didn't think someone would do it. His hand slipped beneath his coat to the walnut handle of the Star PD holstered above his kidney. The man's eyes caught Wager's arm tucked behind him and a hard gleam of laughter came into them. "Now who's nervous, piggy?"

"Maybe we both got reason to be."

"Goddamn you, I didn't kill nobody!"

"Then tell me what you did do."

"I don't have to tell you nothing. There's laws against harassment, even from sons of bitches like you."

"You'll have to go to court to make those laws work, Mauro. I'd like that."

Silence. Across an expanse of frost-killed grass two children shrieked and tumbled down the broad side of one of the geometrical slopes that led down to an empty patio at its bottom. The mother—a long tan coat and blue-and-white scarf—stood at the edge and

212

called something after them. Behind Mauro, the diamonds of the conservatory roof split the sun into sparks of white glare.

"I'll tell you a little story, Mauro, and you tell me if a prosecutor can make a case out of it. A woman's stabbed to death during midday on October 19th. It probably takes place in an apartment—that could be anywhere, couldn't it, Mauro? The killer then cuts off the woman's head. My guess is he did it in a bathtub. It would be a messy job, but you can just wash out a bathtub, right? Hell, just turn on the shower and hose it down. I'll bet you've hosed down a bathtub that way, haven't you, Mauro? The guy leaves her until it's dark. He comes back about midnight, maybe one o'clock, and puts the body in a plastic garbage bag. One of the black ones that everybody has. I bet you have some around your place, don't you? Then—and here it could be the other way around—he dumps the body in an old car in a junkyard, and comes over here with the head. Probably that's in a plastic bag, too, so it don't drip all over; the lab people couldn't find any splash marks anywhere, but the head still drained a little on the sand. You should have seen the sand, Mauro—it stuck together in a kind of wad from the stuff that came out of the neck. Some blood, some other stuff off the brain." He looked at the man, who stood head down and legs spread like a steer clubbed between the eyes. "Pay attention, Nick—here's where it gets exciting. The guy who brought the head into the conservatory had to have a key. There's just no evidence that shows any other way to get inside. But everybody who has a key also has an alibi. Or almost

213

everybody. There's this one guy who says he went to the park at the time the woman was killed, and that he stayed home during the night the body was moved. But he was all alone, Nick; there's nobody to back up his story. Not even the peanut seller remembers. Think about it: one means of entry, one key, one man with no alibi. And a hell of a lot of pressure on the D.A. to nail somebody—anybody—for the crime. What's a prosecutor supposed to do, Nick? Especially if the prime suspect already has a record for violence."

"I didn't do nothing like that, goddamn you to hell!" The thick knuckles whitened on the wooden handle of the trash-pick. "I did not do that!"

"Everybody says they're innocent, Nick. You've been inside—tell me how many innocent victims of justice are inside. And then tell me an ex-con's going to get a break."

The wide head, showing upright bristles and a scattering of gray, still faced the ground. It shook slowly back and forth. "No. I did not do that. No! I did not do that!"

Legs spraddled, he stood almost bending the wooden handle between his broad fists.

"Think how that prosecutor's going to tell that story to some jury. Who do you think that jury's going to believe?" He waited and tried not to look tired. He stood and waited. But the figure was motionless now. 'I'll see you again soon, Nick."

"Again" was the next morning, Wednesday, fifteen days after the killing. Wager yawned and waited along the route that Mauro followed to work. When his rear-view mirror showed the slow figure approach with its slightly waddling stride, he opened the door. Mauro stopped to peer at the car's back window; then the man started past almost at a trot.

"Good morning, Nick."

"Get off my back!"

"It's a public street. Even cops can be in public places just like innocent citizens. Maybe I'll drop by Elton's Place tonight—just to buy you a beer." Wager smiled. "I'll come in every night for a while. Then I'll start missing a few. I'll make it so whenever that door opens, you'll look to see if it's me. Like waiting for the other shoe to drop. Every time that door opens, Nick." Wager tried not to look as if he'd just finished another eight-hour shift; he tried to look happy at the thought of visiting Mauro every night. "Elton's is a nice little bar, almost like home; I'll like it there. If you don't want to see me, you can stay in your room."

"You bastard." Mauro jabbed a thick finger at him. "I been doing some thinking. And you can't lay a thing on me!"

"Tell me your thoughts, Nick."

"I thought about you maybe having a case. And you ain't. It's all circumstantial, Wager—I learned some shit at Buena Vista, and all you got is circumstantial evidence. And there ain't no motive, either! On a heavy charge, things like that work for a defendant, and you know it."

The man was right. He had seen too many juries without the *talangos* to call a guilty bastard guilty unless the evidence was absolute. But more important was Wager's feeling about Mauro—he could be dumb enough to kill, but he wasn't dumb enough to put the head in the place where he worked. Yet he'd lied. "How about an accessory charge? If you know something about the killer and don't tell the cops, you can get nailed for an accessory after the fact."

The grinning face turned away from Wager's eyes, and with the surge of returning worry Mauro's shoulders sagged. "I didn't think of that."

"You're in trouble. All you got to do is tell me what you know and you're out of trouble."

His voice was a whisper: "If I tell, I'm still in trouble."

"What kind?"

"My job, goddamn you! In eight years I get a pension—I lose this job and I lose it all! It ain't much to you, but it's a lifetime to me—a whole lifetime!"

"You're a state employee?"

"Yes."

"When I take you into court, you'll lose your job anyway. Accessory to murder is a felony charge. Felons don't get state pensions."

The wide shoulders sagged more and Wager heard a faint strangled sound deep in the man's throat. But Mauro didn't give up yet, and Wager, now that the end was in sight and the weariness was lifting from him, in a way liked that.

Mauro said, "If I tell you something, you bastard, will you keep me out of it?"

"You tell me. Maybe I can, maybe I can't."

"I want a deal, Wager. I want you to do it so I'm clean."

"I'll see. You did know Rebecca Crowell, didn't you?"

Mauro whispered something.

"What?"

"Yes!"

"When?"

A deep sigh. Wager beckoned him to sit in the car. The heavy body slouched against the creaking seat and he stared through the windshield. "Maybe two months ago now. I didn't know her name, but her and this guy got to talking with me at work. I guess they came to the gardens a few times because they knew what they wanted. But I never noticed them before they talked to me."

"Who was the guy?"

"A photographer. I forget his name. They had this thing about shooting some pictures of her in the conservatory. It sounded like a bunch of shit to me—she said she was a plant freak, and he called her a—I don't know—a 'woods goddess' or some crap. But he paid me a hundred bucks to borrow my key for one night. I was supposed to tell him when the place would be empty—no classes or meetings or things—then I would leave my key in a flowerbox where he could find it. Him and this girl would take the pictures, and put the key back for me to pick up the next day."

"Sumner wouldn't allow him to use the conservatory?"

"No. There's this rule against professional photographers. When Sumner finds out, he'll can me for sure. A whole goddamned lifetime for a shitty

217

hundred bucks."

"Was this for the night of the nineteenth?"

"No. Maybe a month before—six weeks, maybe. A while ago."

"Was the key there the next morning?"

"Yeah." Mauro stopped talking.

"Well?"

"Well what?"

"Is that it? Is that what you've been crapping your pants about?"

"It's my job, Wager! If Sumner finds out that girl had something to do with the gardens, he's going to want to know what. I'll lose my goddamned job because of that!"

"No, you'll lose it for a hundred bucks. What time did you pick up the key that morning?"

Mauro pulled himself back from wherever he'd been watching his pension fly away. "A little after I got to work. Around eleven."

"How were you supposed to let this guy know what night to come?"

"He gave me a number to call."

"Do you still have it?"

"No. But some secretary answered the phone. I think she said it was High Country something."

17

"Yeah," Wager said more to himself than to Mauro, and without surprise, "it would be."

"You think that photographer killed her?"

"I think I'll find out."

"I never even thought about him until you started in on that key." Mauro looked up. "But he returned mine!"

"He had plenty of time to get a duplicate made."

"But the key's got a stamp on it. It says 'State of Colorado—Do Not Duplicate.'"

"Maybe he paid somebody another hundred bucks, Mauro."

"Oh." Mauro picked at his nose with his thumbnail. "Yeah."

Wager started the car. "I'll give you a ride to work."

"Listen, Wager—can you keep me out of it? Please? It's my job! Eight years and I got a pension I can live on. I'm buying a little land down in New Mexico. It's almost clear now—only three more years of payments. If I lose my job, I can't keep up the payments—who's going to hire somebody my age? It's got a fishing stream and lots of trees. You ever been up behind Taos?"

"No."

"God, it's pretty up there. It's two acres on the edge of the national forest, with water and everything. I'm getting a trailer house for it when I retire. A little one's all I need, and I'll be able to afford that. I got it all figured out—eight more years. I can do it—I already done twenty, Wager. Eight years and the pension. You got to keep me out of it! Please!"

He liked the man better when he was fighting than when he was whining. "I'll do what I can."

They arrived at the north side of the conservatory in silence. Mauro opened the door and leaned back into the car. "We got a deal, ain't we? You do what you can to keep me out of it, right?"

"Sure," said Wager.

But his mind was already on Phil Bennett.

In the late-morning sunlight and to his stinging, sleepless eyes, the isolated building containing High Country Profiles and the Electronic Repairs Corporation looked even more stark than at twilight. The parking apron held five or six cars; Wager pulled up at the far end of the row and walked once around the building before entering. The south wall had neither doors nor windows; it was solid brick and caught splinters of bottles and scraps of windblown paper in the high weeds at its base. The west wall bordering the alley had two metal doors, one for each office complex, and a line of four trash drums. There were no windows here, either. He stepped from the alley over a short, leafless hedge to the narrow sidewalk that connected the parking lot with the entry to High Country. Inside the small reception room, with its large photographs covering the walls, a young secretary sat behind her desk. She looked up through thick round glasses and smiled. "What can we do for you?"

"Is Mr. Bennett in?"

"He's at work in the studio. Maybe I can help you."

"I'd just as soon talk to him."

"It'll be about an hour. What'd you want to talk to him about?"

The girl looked about eighteen—a couple of months at a business school, and then to her first job. "I had a few more questions."

She was puzzled. "Questions?"

"Here—I forgot." He pulled out the small leather folder that held his badge and I.D. "I'm Detective Wager." Who wasn't only tired, but now absent-minded. "I talked with Mr. Bennett about Rebecca Crowell . . . Tommie Lee."

"Oh! Wasn't that a terrible thing?" Behind the lenses, her gray eyes widened. She, too, was a pretty girl, and he wondered.

"Have you worked here long?"

"About three months."

"It must be exciting. All the fashion models and such."

"Well, it was at first. But my job's mostly paperwork. That's not very exciting any time."

"Do you do any modeling?"

"Gosh, no!" She laughed. "But I guess that was a compliment. Thanks."

"Is Bennett a good person to work for?"

She suddenly remembered that Wager was a cop. "Yes."

"Are you going to stay with this job?"

"Yes." The eyes behind the lenses said that was an odd question.

Wager sat wearily on the one imitation-leather chair; it was barely deep enough to hold him, but his legs told him it was better than standing. "Do you keep a record of Mr. Bennett's appointments?"

Her hand started for a square brown ledger in a file holder near the telephone. "Yes," she said cautiously.

"Could you look up October 19th and see if Miss Crowell—Tommie Lee—was supposed to be here?"

"I . . . I guess that would be all right."

"Did Bennett tell you not to?"

"No! It's just—well . . ."

"That I'm a cop."

A flush rose up the girl's neck and settled in her cheeks and ears; her hand went to the ledger. "Here." She paused. "Her name's not listed, but there were a lot of cancellations that day. It doesn't say if anyone came in instead. Just a minute." She opened a file drawer bristling with manila folders.

Wager heaved himself to his feet to read the appointment book.

The girl pulled a folder and studied the entries and charges for studio time and proofs. "There's nothing here, either. If she did come in, it was never charged to her account."

On the ledger page titled "Oct. 19" and ruled into hourly blocks beginning at 9 A.M. and ending at 6 P.M., the names were lined out. Most had new dates beside them. Apparently Bennett saw his 10 A.M. customer, and then from eleven on canceled for the rest of the day. "Do these changes happen a lot?"

"Not a lot; it upsets the clients. But sometimes Phil gets behind. If he's got a good session going, he doesn't like to break off just because the time's up."

"Were you here on the nineteenth?"

"Oh, my—what day was that?" She turned back through the loose-leaf calendar on her desk. "That was a Tuesday . . . yes! Now I remember. That was the day the electricity went out. That's why we had all those cancellations!" She flipped back through the ledger, "Just a minute—I remember something about Miss Lee. . . ." She stopped on Monday, October 25th, and ran a finger down the entries. "Here—I found it. See?" She pointed proudly to Tommie Lee's name lined out, with "Stewart, Elaine" printed neatly above it. "I remember she said she was leaving town and wanted to get the work done in time to take it with her. So I called Elaine and she was willing to trade days."

And that explained why the Crowell appointment book had no entry for the day she was killed. "So Miss Lee came in for the ten-o'clock session?"

"I guess so. I usually go out for the doughnuts around then, so I didn't see her." She turned the pages back to the nineteenth. "Maybe she didn't. Maybe that's why her name's not here. But someone was in the studio with Phil when I got back—he had the radio going. He does that when he's working."

"What happened when the electricity went off?"

"It was just before eleven, just about this time. Suddenly all the lights went out and the typewriter stopped." She pointed to the electric machine. "I started to go back to the studio when Phil came out. He was really upset; he hates it when things interrupt his work. And he . . . I guess you could say he yelled at me to cancel everything for the rest of the day. So I did."

"What did you do then?"

"Well, a few minutes later, while I was still on the phone calling the appointments, he came out and apologized." She smiled at Wager. "He was almost crying—he's real emotional; he's a real artist. Phil's like that: he blows up, but he can't stay mad for long. Anyway, he told me I could go to lunch early."

"Do you eat near here?"

"Down at the corner. The Stage Stop Inn. They have a great salad bar."

"Did you come back after lunch?"

"Sure. The electricity was back on, and Phil was in the darkroom. I asked him if he wanted me to call the appointments and tell them to come in, but he said no. He said he could use the time for darkroom work."

"You went into the darkroom to ask him?"

"Yes. Well, not all the way in—no one better go in when the red light's on. I went into the light chamber—that's the little place closed off by the curtains. Phil's been talking about having an intercom put in so I won't have to run back there, but he hasn't gotten around to it yet."

"What did you do for the rest of the day?"

"What I always do—total accounts, mail statements, pay bills, type letters, answer the phone, make appointments. I always have plenty to do. Oh, and Phil let me off early because of the cancellations."

"What time was that?"

"I don't know. A couple hours early."

Plenty of time to move a car, plenty of time to find a junkyard. "Do you get paid enough for all that work?"

She stifled a giggle. "I don't think so. But I'm learning a lot. There's an awful lot that they don't tell you at school."

"Does Bennett give you any extras? Take you out to dinner sometimes?"

Another blush, this one deeper than before. "He has. But that's all."

"What do you mean, 'that's all'?"

"I got a good idea what you're thinking, mister— I've heard the models talking, so I know what you're thinking. And nothing like that's ever happened." Her round chin lifted, and for the life of him, Wager couldn't tell if it was insult at being suspect or insult at being left out. "Anyway, I'm old enough to take care of myself. I pay my own way, and I can do whatever I want to!"

For all her thick glasses, the girl didn't see much. But legally she was right; legally, she was smart enough to run her own life. He sat again and let the silence of the office cool things off. From somewhere beyond one of the partitions at the back of the building came the faint sound of garbled music. The telephone rang and she spoke into it briefly. He thumbed through the pages of his notebook until she hung up. "Does Bennett have clothes for the models to wear?"

"No." She was still sulky. "The models bring their own. There's a dressing room in the studio."

Another five minutes and two telephone calls passed; the girl spun a sheet of paper into the IBM and typed rapidly. Wager shifted once more on the creaking sling of narrow plastic. Finally a latch clicked and two voices splashed out of a back room. A long-legged girl wearing stretch denims said "Bye, Alice," to the secretary, and Bennett stopped still as he saw Wager stand up.

"This man's waiting to see you, Phil."

The photographer nodded; the cap of black hair was clamped over his forehead in a little wave. "It's about Tommie Lee—right, man?"

"Yes. I'm still trying to find out what she did on that last day."

Bennett glanced at Alice, who stared at them. "Come on back. We can rap while I set up for the next session. Alice, shoot the next appointment in as soon as she shows up, honey."

Wager followed him down a short hallway past the darkroom. From the rear, he seemed narrow in the shoulders and walked with a choppy bounce; and Wager noticed that he wore expensive new leather tennis shoes.

The studio was a windowless box whose walls were cluttered with electrical wires, rolls of cardboard, worktables, ladders, fans, and open cabinets filled with filters and bolts of cloth. "Have you glommed onto anything new?" Bennett spoke to a lamp stand he moved toward the large empty platform that filled the center of the area.

"I know a little more than I did. Where she came from, where she worked. But there's no evidence to bring into court."

"Court?" Bennett squinted through the glare of the lamp at Wager. "You mean you got an idea who the dude is?"

"I've got a few leads. But no hard evidence."

Bennett turned off that set of lamps and moved the next forward. Eight stands of horn-shaped bulbs formed a wide circle around the platform. Stiff white paper like some Wager had seen at Tanaka's studio covered the boards. In the ceiling hung a rectangle of two-by-fours slung on a pulley; more lights aimed down from there. "If you got ideas, man, you should be able to get the dude, right?"

"I don't have enough for a probable-cause warrant," said Wager.

"I'm not into what you're saying."

"It means I need more evidence before I've got grounds for a search warrant." That wasn't quite true; officers other than Wager—Ross or Devereaux—could get a warrant because they'd been in homicide long enough to have the court's trust. And Doyle's. But Wager didn't want Ross or Devereaux to get the warrant.

Bennett loosened a clamp and slid a bar of lights halfway down its stand, turned them on, and tightened a flickering bulb. "That sounds weird, man. I mean, if you got a line on the dude, you should be able to bust him."

"Yeah," said Wager. "It should be that way."

The door clattered open and a lithe brunette panted in lugging a small suitcase and a plastic clothes bag. "Phil! I'm sorry I'm late! That damned car wouldn't start again."

"Right, honey; but time's money. You know where to change—I been waiting for you. Let's swing it."

The girl wailed "Oooh" and half ran toward a

227

whitewashed plywood box that shut off one corner of the room.

"They're always late," said Bennett. "And they lay all sorts of hype on me—everything from a stuck zipper to a dying cousin." He shook his head. "I don't know how many cousins have died two or three times. But if you let them get away with it, man, they just get worse and worse."

"Was Tommie Lee late a lot?"

"No, not her. She was one of the few you could set your watch by. She was serious about the program, you know?" He rested a moment on a light stand. "She had everything to be great."

"Some people think different."

"Name one, man!"

"Les Tanaka."

"Aw, he's so full of shit his eyes are brown! That slopehead couldn't tell a real model from . . . from a goddam cemetery angel." Bennett jammed a new bulb into its clamp. "Tanaka can't tell if anybody has talent because he props them up like goddam sandbags and then pisses and moans because they come across like goddam sandbags. Tanaka!"

"O.K., Phil, I'm ready." The brunette came out of the tiny dressing room wearing a silky white evening dress that caught the gleam of lights up and down her long thighs as she walked. Wager watched the cloth stretch tight as she stepped onto the platform, then watched as she slowly turned in the light, winding the cloth down her body like the strokes of long fingers. She saw him and winked.

"Jesus, honey," said Bennett. "Is that what you told

me you were going to wear?"

"Yes—what's wrong with it?"

"Shadows, baby. That kind of cloth is a bitch to get all the shadows out." He shifted two or three stands of lights and switched on the ceiling bank. "But we'll just have to do what we can—right, baby?" Turning to Wager, he smiled. "Sorry to cut you out, man, but business is business. You dig?"

Wager smiled back. "I want to stay. I never saw this kind of work before."

Bennett started to say something, then shrugged. "O.K. with you if this dude stays, honey?" he asked the girl.

"Sure." A wide smile of perfect white teeth shone down on Wager. "I like an audience."

"Yeah, fine—but, baby, keep your attention on me, right? If you're going to stay, man, move back out of the light and we'll try to make like you're not here." He muttered something about tourists and adjusted a few more lights, then moved in with the camera. "O.K., honey, just stand still a minute and let me get some readings."

"My, we're all business today."

"Always, baby, you know that." He held something in his hands and peered at it, then turned off all the lights except those around the platform and the dim workbench near the wall. Then he took more readings. Wager dragged a chair away from the wall.

"Hey, man, keep the fucking noise down!" The photographer sighted half a dozen angles through the camera's viewfinder and went back to the light stands one more time. "O.K., let's get with the program, baby. Let yourself go a little bit; you're about as loose as a goddam telephone pole. Take a deep breath, baby, that's it—now unlax." He fussed and muttered and sighted. "O.K.—now a little live jive and we'll be on our way." He stepped out of the circle of lights and flipped on a radio. The loud blast of a rhythm-and-blues station bounced around the concrete walls while the photographer began swinging his camera around the model like a hovering mosquito.

"Come on, baby—get loose!" He ran around the platform and clicked the trigger. "Give it to me—that's it—gimme, gimme, gimme!" He ran back, the girl bending and pulling against the dress. "Hit me, baby, come on! Lay it on me hard!"

It went through four thumping songs, the last a wailing Negroid voice that Wager heard everywhere and tried to ignore: "When your body thinks it's had enough and it's flopped out flat on the floor, I'm gonna show you what true love is and slip you a little bit more."

Wager watched the shifting, bobbing shape of the photographer gyrate against the twirling, swaying model. Bennett must have been this way with Crowell, too. What was it Ginger Eaton said? That he made a model unfold? He watched the lithe brunette spin and halt, step, stretch—in its way it was a kind of dance. In this woman's mind, maybe even in Bennett's, it was a kind of creation. But, Wager figured, detectives must lack artistic souls, because to him it just looked like a pile of crap.

"O.K., baby, let's break it!" Bennett snapped off the

glaring lamps and rewound the film. In the sudden darkness, the model seemed to shrink. "Honey, you really got to unlax. You're not helping me at all, and I can't do it all by my lonesome. You're supposed to be a model, baby, not a dummy. You can do it, O.K.?"

"I'm sorry, Phil. I'm really trying! But you didn't give me even one minute to catch my breath—I came rushing in and had to rush right through make-up!"

"It's not my fault you were late, honey."

"I told you what happened!"

"All right, all right. Don't blow what cool you got. Get into the negligée and we'll try some skin shots. All you have to do is sit there and breathe deep, O.K.?"

She strode to the dressing room and slammed the thin door. Bennett spread a light-colored quilt on the platform and propped a wide sheet of white paper in a frame as a backdrop. His lips moved, but through the whining clatter of another song, Wager heard no words.

By the time Bennett had the lights rearranged, the girl was back wearing a short pink negligée. It wasn't until she stepped into the glare of the lights that the shadows beneath the cloth told Wager she wore nothing else.

"I want you to relax, now, honey. Just listen to old Phil and move with him, O.K.?"

"I'll try."

"Do better than just try, honey. Do the deed. Hey, I got it—just a minute." He went to the workbench; at one end sat a small refrigerator. "You want some wine?" he called to Wager.

"Sure." He liked full, red wine. But the stuff Bennett poured was white and almost tasteless. Still, it was cold and, in the room's dry heat, good. "Do you give all the models a drink?"

"It depends. It helps them relax. And cools them off so they don't sweat and run their make-up."

He sounded like a dog-trainer. "Did Crowell drink wine?"

"Yeah. She liked a shot or two before we got started. Hey, honey, you didn't eat breakfast, did you?"

"No!"

"Then you want to lose some weight, baby. You're getting a pot."

What looked like a pot to Bennett looked downright skinny to Wager.

"O.K.—lights, camera, action—drink up, honey, and we'll start with some mood shots."

He placed the kneeling model so she sat on her heels, arms and back straight, face turned over her shoulder to the lights, smooth curve of naked buttock peeking beneath the garment's hem. The dark tip on one breast rose tautly under the negligée. "All right, honey, let me see what's on your mind; show it, baby, with the eyes; good, good, a little more with the eyes, now the lips. Sweeten those lips, honey, get them out just a little—lick, baby, lick the lips. O.K., baby, a deep breath and lots of boob, hold it. . . ."

The dance started again; Bennett changed lenses and moved closer, then away, clicking and talking, sometimes singing his instructions to whatever tune blasted from the radio. Wager watched the model through two more changes of clothes—a flaring pants suit with a long scarf that trailed like smoke as the girl spun; a denim outfit that Bennett said looked almost as good as a sack of potatoes. Finally, "O.K., honey, that's it—you done good."

She let out a deep breath and smiled again at Wager, then went to the little dressing room.

Bennett turned out the scorching floodlights and lowered the radio's blare. "Want some more of that?" He pointed to the empty wineglass.

Wager shook his head. "How many sessions do you have in a day?"

"Today, three. I've done as many as six. But, man, there's nothing left when it's over. I mean, people think models do all the work, you know? Maybe they do for dudes like Tanaka; but with me, I get good pictures because I sweat."

The girl came back wearing the denim clothes of her last costume. "When can I see them, Phil?"

"Week after next, honey."

"That's too far off!"

"Baby, I'm buried! I got forty rolls ahead of yours, and a lot of that's finish work."

She tugged at the collar of his open shirt. "Couldn't you just slip mine in? Please?"

He winked at Wager. "They all love me. O.K.—for you, I'll see what I can do. Give Alice a call next week. And burn that denim outfit, honey—it just ain't you."

"Poo!" she said, and kissed him on the cheek; turning another of those very wide smiles on Wager, she was gone in a bustle of make-up kit and clothes bag and the faint aroma of perfume.

Bennett watched the door shut behind her and

shook his head. "Hamburger."

"What?"

"She's like a pound of hamburger—all meat and a little cellophane and nothing else. And she wonders why she can't get big assignments."

"She looked real nice to me."

"Real nice is all right for you, maybe. But for me it's got to be great. If Tanaka was working with her, she wouldn't even look like hamburger. She'd look like shit." He opened the camera and licked a label to stick on the canister of film, then poured himself another glass of wine. "What did you want to ask me?"

That was a good question, and one Wager had tried to concentrate on as the model had turned and breathed deeply and smiled in front of the camera.

"I'm still working on the connection with the Botanic Gardens. I can't see why somebody wanted to do that," said Wager.

"Hey—that was sick. Whoever did that had to be flaky, right?"

"It makes good grounds for an insanity plea."

"Yeah." Bennett held up the film canister. "Let's make this scene in the darkroom, man—time is money."

Wager followed the photographer through the curtained light chamber; the single white bulb in the ceiling of the darkroom was on, but the flat black paint of walls and shelving absorbed its glow. On the far side of the room, Wager saw what he had not found in the studio itself: the fuse box.

"Stand still, man; it takes awhile for your eyes to adjust."

Before Wager could move, Bennett snapped off the overhead light. The sudden darkness was so total that Wager's hands lifted by themselves to push against the solid black. Then he froze; if Bennett still had the knife he used on Crowell, it would be somewhere in this room where the photographer felt at home. Fumbling with one hand for the stability of the doorsill, Wager loosened the automatic holstered at his back. Movement—he heard Bennett moving around. Tennis shoes scraped on the gritty floor; a drawer slid. Wager eased his shoulders along the black wall and tried to listen over the muffled pulse of his own blood. Gradually his blinking eyes felt the red glow of the work light, and in a few seconds he saw Bennett move like a shadow across the dim pink canvass of a print dryer.

"Can you see yet, man? I don't want you bumping into my equipment."

"Me either." Wager's voice squawked and he pumped spittle down the dry walls of his throat. You learn from mistakes, his mind told him; and from another corner of that same mind came the answer: just don't make one mistake too many. Wager felt his way around the wall to the far end of the workbench where Bennett's shape tapped open rolls of film and clipped them into trays filled with developer. He watched the vague form agitate the pans, then carefully move from left to right, rinsing each strip and bathing it in a second solution, then hanging it to dry in a cupboard above the bench. The distance from Wager to the large sink near Bennett was at least six feet; a body could lie there.

"So what's your thing about the Botanic Gardens, man?"

And the darkroom sink would catch the drippings. "Whoever put the head there used a key."

"But there's lot of keys, right?"

"No. In fact, every one's accounted for."

Bennett worked in silence for a few moments. "You're saying you know who used one that night?"

"Everybody who owns a key has a good alibi."

"Oh." He clipped another strip into the drying locker. "That kind of leaves you hanging, doesn't it?"

"Unless there's one more key nobody knows about. Say, a duplicate."

"Is that what you think, man?" Tension raised the pitch of Bennett's voice, and Wager wished he could see the man's eyes.

"What other answer is there?"

"But you got to find that key to prove it, right?"

"I figure it was thrown away. But if I can link Crowell with somebody at the conservatory, I can get a search warrant. And science is wonderful, Bennett."

"I'm not with you."

"A search warrant lets the police lab people in. They can find anything—old blood, for instance. They got a luminol test that brings out bloodstains no matter how much a place has been scrubbed or how long ago."

Through the red glow, the shape silently placed two more strips of film. "You're telling me the killer doesn't have a chance?" It was almost a whisper, like someone talking to hear his own voice just before he jumped.

Wager shifted direction. "Why did Miss Crowell want to be a model so much?"

"Shit! Why does any broad want to be a model? Fame, money, travel, and free soap coupons." Wager studied the silhouette hunched in the redness; it seemed to grip the edge of the bench and stare at the trays of chemical solutions. When it spoke again, the voice was calmer and the jive talk gone. "Most of them don't want to be models—not real ones. They do a couple of shows a month and tell themselves they could have been on top if they really wanted to. It's a goddamned ego trip for them." The figure swayed back and forth at the edge of the workbench. "Very few think it's the only thing in the world. Tommie thought that."

"But she really wasn't that good, was she?"

"Bullshit! I don't care what that fucking Tanaka or anybody else says, she had it! With the right person—with me—she was as good as the best!"

Wager pulled the creased photograph out of his pocket and pressed it flat on the workbench. "Here's one you took of her. She doesn't look much different from any other model."

Bennett squinted at the photograph. "Wait a minute—I can't see a goddam thing." He closed the drying locker and pulled a dark curtain across it, then flipped on the overhead light.

Sudden glare jabbed at Wager's eyes and he blinked away the moisture. But he was glad for the light.

"Yeah. I remember this one. It was one of the first sets we did. And you're right—there's not much to look at, is there?"

"That's what Tanaka said. He told me it wasn't your fault. He said Crowell just wasn't photogenic."

"That son of a bitch doesn't know photogenic from toilet paper! I've got some—" He stopped suddenly.

Wager could see Bennett's pale eyes now, and their pupils were as wide and dark as two holes in the earth. "Let's see those other pictures, Bennett."

18

He held himself poised for whatever Bennett might do. The photographer still gazed at Wager; his mind was working again—Wager could see that in the pale eyes—but what it was saying to the man, he couldn't tell. Bennett slowly turned toward a column of filing cabinets with stacked flat, wide drawers halfway up the wall. "In here," he said hoarsely.

Wager stepped quickly to the hand that reached for a drawer. "I'll do it. You stand right there."

A pile of large color prints lay on the shallow metal tray. The top one was of Rebecca Crowell's face. It was different from any of her that Wager had seen before; the girl's eyes and mouth were less posed, more living: even in the photograph he could almost hear her speak, and the expression called an answering warmth from the heart. Surrounding the face, a green halo of palm fronds, tendrils, broad succulent leaves formed a lush setting that faded into the tangled shadows of a lightless jungle. Both men knew where the pictures had been taken.

"Suppose you tell me about these, Bennett." Wager's voice seemed suddenly to slice some kind of leash; the photographer lunged at the light switch and the room fell black as Wager, dropping to hands and knees, tumbled to the right. His last glimpse of Bennett showed the man reaching for something bulky on a shelf near the door. Holding his breath and himself motionless on the cold concrete, Wager listened for a gasp, for a footstep, a scrape—anything. But only silence. Bennett was at home in the darkroom and he was in no hurry. Wager eased to a crouching position that he hoped faced the killer and tried silently to slip his hand beneath his coat to the pistol waiting there.

Then he heard something: a murmur. "What'd you say, Bennett?"

"You want to hurt me."

"No." It came from just over there, near the door, near the light switch. His eyes watered slightly as they strained to see through the dull red of the blackout light. Perhaps that shadow, the low bulky one... "Bennett?"

He was hit from the side by something heavy and metal, the blow splitting through the red in a flash of yellow and knocking him flat against the gritty floor. A numbness lay against skull and shoulder, and in his ears was that high-pitched buzz that comes with being hit hard. Rolling over frantically, he dug at the holster with his left hand but the pistol was gone, fallen from his numb fingers. A shadow moved at the edge of vision and he kicked a heel into the swirling red and felt the solid jar of contact, heard a wheezing grunt from somewhere under the looming tower of the enlarger as Bennett swore and dropped the metal thing he had used as a weapon. A second later, fingers jabbed at Wager's face, ripping down his ear and slicing toward his eyes. Wager twisted back and away, rolling out of the grip and clubbing wildly at the figure blotting the red light, missing, twisting to pull his useless arm away from the grunting swarm of darkness leaping at him.

Bennett hit at him again, the red bulb sparkling on the cluster of tripod legs that whistled slightly as they whipped toward him. Wager kicked once more, able to see the man's outline now, able to make out arms and legs and crotch, able to aim his heel and drive his whole weight behind the shaft of his leg.

Bennett's shriek covered the splintering bottles knocked tumbling from a cabinet and Wager grasped in the dark beneath the workbench for the writhing man, pulling him across the glass and concrete into the faint red glow, grabbing his hair to smack his head solidly against the floor and then straddle the bucking, twisting chest of the photographer.

"You're hurting me! You want to kill me!"

"You're goddamned right I do!" Wager smacked the skull once more. "And I sure as shit will if you don't lay still!"

Wager used his car radio to send the 10-95—subject in custody. It crossed his mind to go past Denver General Hospital and have the bloody-headed photographer checked over; but the son of a bitch didn't hurt any more than he did, and only now could Wager move his right arm enough to shift gears. In the rear seat, handcuffs looped beneath the back of his fashionably wide leather belt, Bennett grunted and sat doubled, pressing his sore testicles between clamped legs. At the end of the sidewalk, the secretary, Alice, held both fists over her mouth and stared silently at them with eyes enormous behind her thick lenses.

Wager pulled into traffic and gave the grunting man his rights as he steered with one hand and squinted through the throb of his skull. The numbness was wearing off to leave an aching pulse at the juncture of his neck and shoulder, and a tingling that was almost painful down the outside of his hand. "You hear what I just said, Bennett?" He gingerly twisted the rear-view mirror so it showed the photographer's pale face and blood-matted cap of black hair.

"Yes."

"Now you tell me about Rebecca Crowell."

". . . Yes."

They reached the police building a little before noon; homicide's day shift was on the street, and Wager and Bennett had the office to themselves. He marched the stiff-legged photographer to a desk just out of sight of the busy corridor and unlocked the cuffs. "You sit here and don't try no more shit on me." He pulled a legal tablet out of a drawer and pushed it and a ball-point pen at Bennett. "You write what I tell you." He dictated the first couple of sentences. "You understand that?"

The grunting had stopped and now the voice was just weary. "Yes."

"Good. Now you write down everything you told me on the way over here."

Detectives from the other divisions of the bureau, following the whisper that somehow spreads whenever a homicide suspect confesses, stuck their heads in to glance at Bennett and raise their eyebrows at Wager.

"That's him?" one muttered.

"Yes."

"Looks like you dropped the hammer on him."

"He didn't feel like coming in."

The detective's eyes followed something along Wager's cheek. "You better get that looked at—it's deep."

The whisper finally reached Doyle. He stood silently in the doorway and looked at the man who slowly wrote on the pad of lined yellow paper. "I want to talk to you, Wager. In the hall." The bulldog's jaw shoved toward him. "What the hell did you do to that prisoner?"

"He resisted arrest."

"You got any witnesses?"

"Only the scars." Wager pointed to his cheek. "And one damned bad headache, Chief Doyle."

The bulldog shook his head. "It still stinks. Did you call for a doctor to look at him?"

"Not yet."

"I'll do it." Doyle went to his own office.

Wager drew a cup of water from the cooler and took one to Bennett, who now sat without writing. "You finished already?"

"Yes." The man's narrow shoulders sloped even more and he looked at the cut on Wager's face. "You know—I don't even remember fighting with you. It was just like Tommie. . . . I don't really remember." The pale eyes were wide with innocence.

Sure he didn't remember. Wager spun the pad to read over the short passage of shaky handwriting. The confession began with the familiar dictated sentences: "I have been advised of my rights and warned that anything I say might be used against me in a court of law. I make the following statement in my own hand and of my own free will." Then Bennett's words started: he and Tommie Lee had a photography session around noon on October 19th. They argued about her leaving, and nothing he said could make her change her mind. He wasn't sure what happened next. He remembered seeing the knife beside the platform in the studio; he kept it around for cutting heavy paper. He remembered setting his camera down and grabbing the knife. He must have stabbed her, but he did not remember much until he kind of woke up in the darkroom and saw what he had done.

"This is all you want to say?"

The narrow shoulders lifted once and fell. "What more is there?"

There wasn't much more that was needed, but a lot more that Wager wanted. "Sign here and put today's date—November 3rd." Bennett signed; then Wager signed and dated it as witness. "Was she wearing a nightgown when you stabbed her?"

Through the lines of weariness and lingering nausea, Bennett was surprised. "Yes. She bought it for that session." He massaged his crotch. "God, she was beautiful—not like that broad you saw today, but beautiful!" His gaze shifted to the brown wall of the office. "It was like that session in the conservatory. I made her beautiful. I knew it was there, and I found it."

"What did you do with the clothes and the knife?"

"I buried them in the trash can in the alley after dark. I was scared by then. I knew what I'd done by then."

"Why'd you put her head in the conservatory?"

Bennett's pale eyes swiveled his way, but Wager could not tell what the photographer was looking at. "I brought her to life there. That was where I made her live!"

"You took her head to the conservatory at about two in the morning, is that right?"

The pale eyes blinked and Bennett was back now to gaze at Wager. "I don't remember cutting it off. I just sort of woke up and looked down and she was . . . in the sink. So I took her to the spot where she was beautiful. I was sorry. I told her I was sorry."

"You had a duplicate of Mauro's key?"

"Mauro? That's the name of the guy at the conservatory? Yes. I had one made so Tommie and I could go back. . . ." He sighed. "You want all that written down, too?"

A deal was a deal, even with Mauro. "No. Why'd you dump her body in that car?"

The question took a second or two to work through Bennett's thoughts; then his eyes turned milky with the haze of pure hate. "What fucking good was it any more!"

Doyle came in and muttered that the doctor would be by in a while.

"Were you lovers? Bennett—were you and Tommie lovers?" asked Wager.

He focused his gaze like a stiletto point on him. "What?"

"Were you and Rebecca Crowell lovers?"

"Yeah." The photographer blinked two or three

times and sucked in a deep breath. "That's kind of funny."

"How, funny?"

"She wasn't worth a shit in bed. I've had a lot better." Another deep breath and he turned to Doyle, explaining. "It was more than screwing. Nobody knew what she had but me. I found it—I made her live! And then she said she didn't want to waste any more time in this town."

"Or with you?" asked Doyle.

"She didn't say that. But that's what she meant."

"Haven't you ever left anybody?" asked Wager.

"*I* left *them*. There's a big difference."

Wager leaned forward, his hand rubbing gently at the hot swelling of bruised muscle in his neck. "What did she say that made you do it?"

Bennett, too, was tired and hurt. He straightened and winced against the pull of his sore groin. "You figured that out, too, didn't you? Yeah." He shook his head. "After all that—after that wonderful birth of life in all that greenness and heat of the garden, and then being able to re-create the same thing right there in the studio.... You really know what it was? I wanted so much for her to stay—I never before asked anybody to stay. I even begged!" Another shake of the head. "She just told me to finish the session. She said she wanted the proofs ready before she left town. And then that bitch smiled for the camera!"

Doyle grunted. "And that's when you did it."

Bennett looked at him and then at Wager and then at a corner of the office floor where someone had kicked a mashed cigarette butt. His voice rose in pitch nd the jive talk returned. "I don't remember exactly, man. Like I said, things got pretty fuzzy in my head bout that time." Bennett's face lost a few of the lines hat had been there a moment ago. "I must of flipped ut, you know? The next thing I remember is being in he darkroom after it was all over." He shook his head. "Man, I must of blown so far out I was in orbit!"

Innocent by reason of insanity. Wager could hear a awyer's voice make that plea: "Your honor, my client as freely confessed to the crime, but the evidence learly demonstrated that the act was not premedi- ated, and that at the time of committing said act, Mr. Bennett was not of sound mind. Surely, your honor, he subsequent mutilation of the victim is prima facie vidence of an unbalanced state of mind." Surely.

The prosecutor would buy that plea. It saved work, t saved the court's time, it served justice—more or ess. And, in a way, there was truth to it.

Because, as Wager thought back over what he'd earned of Rebecca Crowell and the people whose ives had mixed with hers, Bennet seemed only a mall part of an insane world. And maybe even the victim shared that insanity.

"Here comes the doc," said Doyle. "When he's hrough with the prisoner, I want him to look at you."

A uniformed officer accompanied the doctor into he office. "Is this the one? Take off your shirt, please. Let's see how bad it is."

"It's not just the shirt, man." Bennett painfully tood and began unbuttoning.

The bulldog led Wager down to his office and drew a cup of coffee from his private stock. "Here. We'll get a warrant for the lab to go over that studio for hard evidence in case the confession's thrown out."

"I did not beat it out of him."

"That's not what the defense will say. And that's why I want the doc to look at you, too."

Wager should have guessed it wasn't just because he hurt.

"I don't know how you got a lead on Bennett, Wager. But you did all right."

He knew that. "Yes, sir."

"Don't go get the big head, though. Your partner comes back the day after tomorrow, and you've got a lot to learn about proper procedures."

"Yes, sir."

"I suppose you've heard about your friend Gargan?"

"No."

"He was picked up early Tuesday morning. On a tip. Speeding, reckless driving, six counts of running a stop sign, failure to yield the right of way, driving under the influence, evading arrest, disturbance, use of filthy language, interference with an officer, resisting arrest, and threatening an officer."

"My, my."

"If he hadn't been so drunk, he could have gotten off with a warning because he's a reporter." The bulldog looked at him. "But he started handing out all this crap about a big story and some police conspiracy to keep the press away to protect somebody important. You wouldn't know anything about that?"

"Why should I?"

"He mentioned your name in passing."

"We had a drink or two. I thanked him for the nice story he did on me." Wager smiled. "And if he was that drunk, I wouldn't trust his memory too much."

Doyle's lower teeth showed in what may have been a smile a little like Wager's. "That's what I figured."